Seraf

COSMIC
CONUNDRUM

Serafina Loves Science!

COSMIC CONUNDRUM

Cara Bartek, Ph.D.

Absolute Love Publishing

Absolute Love Publishing

Cosmic Conundrum

A book by Absolute Love Publishing

Published by Absolute Love Publishing
USA

Illustration by Logynn Hailley

ISBN-13: 978-0-9995773-3-2
United States of America

By Cara Bartek

Cosmic Conundrum
Quantum Quagmire

Dedication

To my CC, the original Serafina Marina Sterling

Praise for Cosmic Conundrum

"Through the quirky character of Serafina, *Cosmic Conundrum* shows us that science can be fascinating! Girls, you can embrace your curiosity, follow your passions, and most importantly, just be you! As an environmental scientist, I love this series!" - *Emily Thompson, Edwards Aquifer Authority Environmental Scientist*

"Every opportunity for inquiring girls to stretch their STEM skills and reach for new horizons is time well spent. The unique characteristics of the exceptional in-between-agers portrayed in Serafina Loves Science! will certainly strike a chord with the readers, and Serafina's adventures are sure to inspire new ideas and open new pathways of creativity." - *Rick Varner, Scobee Education Center Director*

"This book is fabulous! It made me laugh out loud a few times. My niece Sadie said she loves that Sera has GRIT! This is a true example of how we can let bullying define us or inspire us. I also loved that it makes science fun! I cannot wait for the sequel!" - *Rebecca Boenigk, Neutral Posture CEO*

"*Cosmic Conundrum* is an excellent book for all students. It is about Serafina's love of science and her adventures in pursuing her dream. The book is full of science information from the perspective of a young girl and also addresses several issues common to our youth, including friendship, loyalty, facing one's fears, pursuing one's dreams, and dealing with bullies. I highly recommend this book for young readers, especially girls. *Cosmic Conundrum* is an exciting and entertaining story that will give girls confidence to pursue science careers." - *Miguel Sepulveda, school counselor and STEM Coordinator*

"*Cosmic Conundrum* is a book for all ages, a timeless story about humanity and kindness with a technological twist of events. Fascination with science and space exploration leads Serafina, a precocious thinker and oblivious-to-girlie-things 11-year-old, to a space adventure camp. Will she make friends? Will she win the top prize for her invention? Will she be chosen to be a junior astronaut? Mixed emotions surge when the unexpected happens to Serafina." - *Lidya Kushner Osadchey, business consultant, executive coach, parent, and community leader*

CONTENTS

HELLO!

My name is Serafina Sterling, and I love science! Love may seem like a strong word for something that isn't warm or fuzzy or flavored like a jelly bean, but love is the only accurate word I can use to describe the feeling I have about science. You see, science is like putting on a pair of new glasses after years and years of seeing everything blurry. It brings things into focus. It straightens the wavy edges and makes it all vibrant. That's important when you're trying to figure things out, like most kids are. And while I admit science doesn't have all the answers to life's major questions (like what exactly "fleek" means and the most appropriate time to use such an adjective), it provides some much-needed context. Science helps me understand the world, like why the sky is blue and how chubby, little caterpillars turn into beautiful butterflies. Of course, not everyone loves science as much as I do.

My aunt, Celeste, calls herself a flower child. She doesn't love science as much as she loves the sixties. She wears bell bottoms and sunglasses with round, blue lenses on the tip of her nose and grows her hair out way past her waist even though she's, like, really old, probably 30 or 40. Most of the time, I try to ignore all of the weird hippie things she does, like burning incense and setting her neighbor's dogs free so they can live among their "wolf brethren," but one thing I can't ignore about my aunt is her music. She plays this one song, "People are Strange," over and over, and it always gets stuck in my head. I can't help but agree with the sentiment. You see, there is one part of the world that science has yet to fully explain: people. Because, of course, people *are* strange.

This is a story about people. This is a story about me trying to understand people, in particular a bunch of 11-year-old kids at a space adventure. While I do have a vast working knowledge of the noble gases, one thing I have no clue about is what makes other kids tick. Especially space-crazed kids who spend an entire week away from their parents and eat contraband candy like it's ... like it's ... candy. This is a story about how I use that one thing that I love more than popcorn-flavored jelly beans: SCIENCE!

CHAPTER ONE

"Georgia, Georgia," I said in a breathless voice. "Georgia Weebly, come in!" This time I screeched the words and pressed my face close to the screen.

"Sera, Sera. Calm down. I need you to slow down and move your face away from the screen. This is FaceTime, not a walkie talkie," Georgia replied.

I moved the screen of Mom's tablet away from my face and took a breath, trying to compose myself. It didn't work.

"Georgia!" I screamed again. "I need your label maker! Hurry!"

Georgia blinked behind her big, pink glasses and arched her eyebrows. "What?"

I looked down at the bright green package from the Musgrave Space Institute and smiled. It was not your normal smile. It wasn't the gentle pull that tugs your lips into a lazy curl. It was not the kind of smile you give to teachers when they ask if you know the difference between a stable and unstable chemical compound. (Of course I know the difference!) It wasn't the kind of smile that says that small, teeny, tiny, explosion in chemistry lab was a complete accident, *honest.*

Nope. This was the kind of grin that made my eyes nearly close shut and my cheeks cramp. This was the kind of smirk that started somewhere near my left ear and went almost to my right shoulder. It was massive! It was huge! It was so painfully large and giant that my teeth started to dry out.

Georgia's forehead wrinkled. "Why do you need a label maker so bad? What's going on with you?" She paused, and then her eyes sparkled. "Oh!" she shrieked, fluttering her hands and grinning with excitement. "All those years of me telling you the joys of organization have finally paid off! You want to get organized! No more living in filth!"

I recoiled at Georgia's words. My smile faded.

Yes, I had a tendency to be on the messy side, but I didn't think I was that bad. I scrunched my nose and quickly surveyed my room. My bookshelf overflowed with books. My dresser drawers looked like they had exploded; shorts, t-shirts, and underpants spilled onto the floor.

Disorganized? Sure. I was disorganized, especially compared to Georgia, with her color-coded coordination and labeled storage bins, but *filthy?* I wasn't filthy! I only saw one banana peel amongst the chaos … and one empty soup can.

When did I eat corn chowder? I wondered.

"No." I turned back to the tablet. "No, no, no. You don't understand what's happening here."

Georgia pushed her glasses up on her nose. "Then enlighten me, Serafina."

I took another deep breath and straightened my shoulders. "I got into Musgrave Space Adventure!" My face-splitting smile returned. "It's the best news ever!"

It was. The Musgrave Space Adventure was not an ordinary space adventure. It was the Ivy League of space adventures, founded by the great scientific entrepreneur Jeronimo Musgrave himself. *The* Jeronimo Musgrave! The man who, legend has it, personally greeted visitors from space and studied a real-life space ship while working at the Los Alamos Laboratory in New Mexico in 1995.

Some said his alien interaction actually changed his DNA, like when that radioactive arachnid bit Spider-Man. Others said his brain was sucked out through his ear and replaced with a super-advanced, extraterrestrial, supercomputer brain. Of course nothing has ever been confirmed, but his accomplishments do seem superhuman. I mean, this man, this *genius* brought jet-engine minivans to the suburbs!

After Jeronimo left Los Alamos, he founded Jeronimo's Jets where he modified regular cars by reinforcing their chassis with steel girders and installing a secondary engine in the back: a jet engine! With just a flip of a switch, boring old sedans flew down the highway at speeds that had never been clocked. The government shut it down, of course, after several traffic accidents and an incident involving a mom, a button-pushing toddler, and a carpool lane at school (no one was hurt but several orange traffic cones were flattened), but Jeronimo didn't let that get him down.

Instead, he founded a super-progressive robotics company that took his love for supercharging plain-jane cars and turned it toward everyday things: ovens that baked a pie and fired pottery at the same time, autoclaves that let hospitals sterilize surgical instruments at lightning speeds, and dishwashers that killed harmful microbes *and* took the pattern off of Grandma's china!

The man was a certified genius. He had more than 300 patents under his belt, and had been named the American entrepreneur of the year four years in a row. While green Mohawks weren't really my style, it was nice to see someone who was not afraid to be who he wanted to be on the cover of 100 major magazines. And the space adventure was his best idea yet.

For the past three years, Jeronimo had been working on something way more awesome—and way more amazing—than mutant dishwashers: building spaceships. Even better, he'd pledged to bring a manned mission to Mars by 2030. To get there, he just needed young, passionate, and brave future cosmonauts who he could train in his very own Musgrave Space Institute.

Six months earlier, Jeronimo had issued an open call to all scientists under the age of 13 to apply for 50 open spots for a grueling scientific competition to see who could earn a coveted spot in his junior astronaut development program. The application had been killer. Wannabe astronauts had to submit notarized transcripts; a 10-page autobiography complete with philosophical stances on such topics as politics, the environment, and the role of the Kardashian family in modern society; a DNA sample; a fully executed last will and testament; and an original working invention designed to make space travel more bearable.

I had struggled for months trying to think of an invention. While space food definitely left something to be desired—it looked like cat food squeezed out of a toothpaste tube—at least you got to eat it while performing backflips in midair. That seemed bearable enough, even if those flips were just about the only real activities you could enjoy in the shuttle. NASA had the water and pooping things down pretty well, too, so I was at a loss. Until it hit me: The hardest part of space travel would be missing everyone back home.

"You got in? You got into the Musgrave Space Adventure?" Georgia's eyes grew wide and her mouth opened. She pressed her palms to the side of her face and began to scream at the top of her lungs.

I couldn't help it. I screamed, too. A super-sonic, high-pitch blast flowed from my belly button all the way to Georgia's face. My belly quivered, and my lungs ached.

From downstairs, my wiener-beagle, Madame Curie, begin to howl. I must have been hitting that perfect doggie pitch that made her point her head toward the sky and howl like a wolf.

"Woooooo! Woo, woo, woooooo!" she bayed.

"Ahhhhhhhh!" Georgia screamed.

"Ahhhhhhhh!" I screamed.

From outside, the neighborhood dogs joined in. Madame Curie's cry incited a neighborhood riot. I heard deep Great Dane howls, and medium Labra-Doodle howls, and tiny Chihuahua howls coming from all directions.

My door flew open.

"Serafina," my mom said, hands on her hips, "I know you're excited, and I am, too. But you can't go on screaming like this for the rest of the day. The neighbors are going to start complaining."

"Sorry, Mom," I said sheepishly.

"Sorry, Mrs. Sterling," Georgia said as she flung her blonde curls over her shoulder.

I spun the screen toward Mom so she could see Georgia's face.

Once our screams stopped, so did the doggie howls.

Mom walked closer. "Hello, Georgia. How are you? How's your mother?"

"Great," Georgia said politely.

Mom smiled. "Good. Now listen, girls. No more screaming. I mean it. You've whipped Madame Curie into a frenzy." She narrowed her eyes in my direction.

"Sorry," I said quietly.

Mom came closer to the screen and looked directly at Georgia. "Georgia, you're welcome to come over later. We are having a barbeque. We've got some brisket and ribs on the smoker. Bring your family."

"Sounds great, Mrs. Sterling," she said, "but I have

one question."

"Yes?"

"By any chance is this a vegan brisket? The reason that I ask is because I have been seriously exploring living a cruelty-free life and am concerned about factory-raised meat. Especially beef."

Mom shook her head. "No, Georgia. No vegan beef here."

Georgia shrugged her shoulders. "Just thought I'd ask. No biggie. I already had a Big Mac today so I'm not making any permanent changes just yet. But I will definitely be using cruelty-free body lotion."

Mom chuckled. "Body lotion? Well, I'm glad you stand by your morals." She waved goodbye and left the room.

I turned the screen back toward myself.

"I'm so happy for you!" said Georgia.

I smiled. "Thanks!"

Georgia pulled a pad from her back pocket and began to make notes.

"What're you doing?" I asked, trying to zoom in on her notes.

"Just a sec," Georgia said, scribbling some more. Then she looked up at me and once again pushed her glasses up on her nose. "I'm making a list of things you will need." Then she pulled out her label maker and began to inspect it. "Batteries full, and we're good on label tape."

"I don't know what to bring," I moaned.

"Well aren't you glad you have me, Serafina? I know exactly what you need!"

CHAPTER TWO

As Georgia's parents and mine laughed on the back patio and tended to the non-vegan beef, Georgia and I sat upstairs in my room. Georgia consulted her list, which was long and written in several different colors of ink, and scrunched her nose at the clothes I had laid out on my bed.

"Sera," she said, once again pushing her glasses up her nose, "I'm not seeing a lot of coordination in your wardrobe."

I shrugged my shoulders. "Okay."

She placed her pad and bright green pen on the bed. "You see, this"—she pulled a pair of bright yellow jeans from the pile and held them up—"is a very bold color."

I nodded my head. It seemed like a fairly obvious statement. "Yeah ..."

"I've seen you wear these jeans on more than one occasion." She turned her head slightly toward me, gazing out of only one eye while keeping the other one on my bright yellow jeans.

I furrowed my brow. "Okay ..." I said again,

sounding like Mom when I ask her about hypothetical radiation exposure.

"You see this is a very nice shade of yellow. It really is, but—"

I cut her off. "Spit it out, Georgia. Just say what you need to say."

Georgia tilted her head and pursed her lips in her I'm-the-most-organized-and-coordinated-kid-in-all-of-middle-school kind of way. "Ahem," she cleared her throat. "What I am saying is that bold colors should really be the *center* of any outfit choice."

Confused and losing patience, I snorted. "So!"

"So! So you can't wear your bright green Christmas sweater, complete with tinsel tree and working lights, with these pants. Especially not in July!"

I tilted my head. "So it's a seasonal thing?"

"It's a style thing!" she shouted and grabbed her head. Her blonde curls pointed in every direction. "Serafina, you have the worst style! You need my help!"

Her delivery was poor, but Georgia was right. I did have the worst style. But it wasn't because I didn't understand the intricacies of the color spectrum. I knew tons about the wavelengths in the visible spectrum and even the infrared. What I didn't know was how those wavelengths went together. More importantly, I didn't care. When it came to fashion choices, my tastes had a tendency to track toward the convenient. I was usually too busy trying to understand the morphology of a walking stick, or working up a plan to re-animate an army of road kill raccoons to keep my older and much lamer brother Apollo out of my room, to worry about matching colors. Most days, I was lucky to have on a pair of matching shoes before I left the house.

"Why does it matter, Georgia?" I groaned.

"Because," she said as she dug around in her pocket, "you are trying to make an impression on these people. You are trying to win a spot in the junior astronaut development program."

"That's true, but my skills will carry me through." I tossed my hands in the air. "It doesn't matter what I'm wearing!"

Georgia pulled out her smart phone and began to tap the screen. "That may be true, Serafina. Your skills are awesome, and I know you can rock it. But people do judge a book by its cover."

I huffed and crossed my arms over my chest. "Well, that's stupid."

Georgia continued to type and swipe. "That's true, too," she conceded, "but it doesn't make appearance any less important. People can be shallow. I mean, I don't mind the snow boots in summer but other people might think you are—"

"Are what?" I interrupted. I looked down and noticed that I had one pink snow boot on my left foot and one well-worn, white Chuck Taylor on my right. While I was a little disappointed that I was wearing mismatched shoes and making Georgia's points all the more valid, I was happy to see the high top. I had thought I'd lost it!

Georgia pinched her lips together. I could tell she

was holding back.

"Are *what*, Georgia?" I stood up and put my hands on my hips.

She shrugged her shoulders and held her palms up. "I don't know. Just forget I said it."

"Oh, no. Now I need to know. They will think I'm what?" I tapped my snow boot on the ground.

Georgia looked at my tapping foot and sighed. "Weird," she said in a barely audible whisper.

"What?" I shouted. "Weird? They will think I"—I poked my thumb into my chest—"am *weird*?"

Georgia cocked her head to one side and smirked. "Strange. Odd. Geek. Dweeb. Loser. Oddball. Freak. Other synonyms you know. They all mean the same thing."

"No. No way," I said, waving my hands at my waist. "Are you forgetting I'm going to space adventure? This isn't a beauty pageant. I'm going to be learning about rockets, and planetary orbits, and what you do if you need to poop in a space suit."

"Just hear me out." Georgia held her phone to my face. "Do you see her?" She pointed to the screen.

I looked where she was pointing. There was an image of what looked like a full-grown woman clad in acid-washed jeans and a ratty, old t-shirt that read "Science Gal." Her jet-black hair was pulled into a perfect bun that sat on top of her perfect head. Her eyebrows were thick and black and her eyes a deep brown. She was scowling at the camera in a way that said, "Don't mess with me." The typical supermodel look.

"Who is that?" I asked. "Is that the evil math tutor you've been taking about?"

"What?" Georgia looked and then twisted the screen back toward me. "That's Ida Hammer. She's 12. My math tutor is 25."

"Well, she looks 25. Twenty, for sure. Anyway, who is *Ida Hammer*?"

"Your competition."

Georgia must have seen the confusion on my face because she launched directly into an explanation. "Ida Hammer is the most amazing chick in science right now. Her dad is a cancer researcher, and her mom is a Nobel Prize winning mathematician. Ida was literally raised on science. She has her own theorem! I heard that her nanny was a top Russian physicist who started drilling her before she could even walk. Ida has received early acceptance to Stanford, Yale, and MIT. Harvard is still holding out because she has yet to make a break though on her cold fusion project. She has like a million followers on Instagram and Twitter and even has a personal assistant. She announced yesterday that she was accepted to Musgrave, too."

My mouth gaped open.

"And, *look*. Her style is impeccable." Georgia gazed lovingly at the screen. "Those jeans are amazing."

"Forget the jeans," I said, grabbing the phone. "A million followers on social media? My mom won't even let me have a phone."

I began to scroll through Ida's posts. I saw a picture of her standing between Neil deGrasse

Tyson and Stephen Hawking in front of the CERN accelerator complex in Geneva. The caption read, "Just hanging with my homies, Neil and Steve. #finallysomeintelligentconversation."

The next photo was Ida in a suede lab coat in a lab, with the caption "#justfindingacureforthecold #allinadayswork." I stopped scrolling when I saw a photo of Ryan Gosling asking her for an autograph that was captioned, "#heygirlcanyousignthis #allmyadoringfans."

I slammed Georgia's phone down. "She can't be for real."

Georgia shrugged again, this time with a little more sympathy. "She is, and I hear she's brutal. Like doesn't-take-any-prisoners kind of brutal. She wins everything she's in and isn't afraid to spill a little blood." Georgia made a slashing motion across her throat.

I gulped. "I just wanted to put some labels in my underpants."

Georgia patted my shoulder. "Of course you did."

I turned to Georgia. "How am I supposed to compete with the ... the ... wrench?"

Georgia gave me a confused look and then smiled. "Oh no, Serafina. Her name is Ida Hammer. *Hammer.* Not wrench."

I screamed. "AHHHHHHHH!"

Georgia covered her ears with both hands. "Jiminy Christmas. I didn't mean to make you upset."

"Why couldn't you just stick to label making?"

Georgia shrugged again.

"How exactly am I going to compete with someone like Ida Hammer?"

Georgia pursed her lips in a sympathetic gaze. "Sera. With someone like Ida Hammer, there is no competition. She is the total package. Beauty, brains, and a highly marketable social media presence."

I put my head in my hands and fell backward on my bed. "What did I get myself into? I thought this was going to be about jet propulsion, not matching my belt to my shoes and learning how to read all of those long hashtag words."

Georgia shook her head disapprovingly. "Trending," she corrected, "and you don't even own any belts."

I threw up my hands. "Way to rub it in!" I shrieked.

"Listen, Serafina. What I'm trying to tell you is that to be competitive at a place like Musgrave you can't just be smart." She began listing on her fingers. "You have to have style. You have to have a handle. Do you Snapchat?"

I sighed and buried my face once again in my hands. "I don't even know what that is."

Georgia shook her head again. "Well, you better start learning." She picked up my electric Christmas tree sweater. "And get rid of this hideous sweater."

CHAPTER THREE

It was finally time! My parents and I had bundled into the car early that morning, and we were on our way to the Musgrave Institute in Houston. It was my dream finally coming true—I was going to meet Jeronimo Musgrave and work on a real spaceship!—but I didn't feel as excited as I knew I should. As I watched the skyline of downtown draw closer and closer, I couldn't stop thinking about Isaac Newton.

All space enthusiasts owe a serious debt to Isaac Newton and not because of his awesome hair that kind of looks like a manly beehive. Isaac rocked it because of his super-important observations about the world, specifically his three laws about the physical world. They aren't like normal laws that police officers enforce, like always wear a seatbelt. These laws lay the foundation for how we understand gravity and motion and how to get rockets into space. Newton's laws state a principle or basic truth about the way the world operates.

Some of my teachers have said that Newton came to his conclusion after an apple smacked the top of his manly beehive. Others have said that story is pure fantasy. Either way, the legend said that Newton was sitting under an apple tree all dreamy-eyed and pensive about gravity when a giant, red apple bopped the top of his head with no warning. The smack must have knocked something loose in his brain. He took one look at the head-smacking apple and wondered, "Why do apples fall to the ground?" Shortly thereafter, Newton identified the universal force called gravity, the force that makes apples fall, and began uncovering three of the most important scientific laws ever written.

His first law kept running through my head. The law states that an object at rest has a tendency to stay at rest and an object in motion tends to stay in motion. It's pretty simple. If I placed a marble on a perfectly flat, perfectly level surface like a kitchen table, then the marble would stay right where I put it. It wouldn't go anywhere because there would be no other forces acting on it. This could and would change if something, like an outside force, acted upon it. If a second marble were rolling around on the table and struck the perfectly still marble, then the still marble would start rolling around, too. See? Simple!

The same principle would apply if the first marble was rolling gently in one direction and a second marble came careening from the side and smacked it off course. The rolling marble would have kept rolling in a straight line except another force acted upon it: a wild marble. Georgia was *my* wild marble.

If it hadn't have been for Georgia, I would have

been ecstatic that morning instead of worried about Ida Hammer. I would have been gently resting on my flat surface of space adventure calm.

It wasn't that Ida Hammer intimidated me. Well, okay. She did. That was exactly my problem.

I'd been fantasizing about space exploration since I was a kid, like two or three years old. I'd imagined walking the surface of the moon and drawing my initials in the moon sand. I'd thought about landing my rocket on the red surface of Mars and waving my space glove back at Mom and Dad. As the first person to ever walk on Mars, I would say something profound like, "One small step for middle schoolers, one giant leap for tween kind." Then I would take the most epic selfie ever.

Earning a spot in Jeronimo's highly coveted junior astronaut development program would make those dreams come true. Sadly, all I could think about was Ida and her one million followers and perfect style.

"We're here, girl squirrel," Dad said, interrupting my thoughts.

"Are you nervous?" Mom asked. "You're so quiet."

I pursed my lips and closed my eyes. "Yep. Just nervous."

I felt Mom patting my knee. "There's no reason to be nervous. You're going to have a great time. Try to relax."

I opened my eyes and looked at her smiling face. Parents can be so naïve sometimes. They have no idea the pressures an 11-year-old faces these days.

"Let me help you with your bag," Dad said as he

reached for my suitcase.

I pressed my face against the van's window, trying to get a better look at the other kids. I saw what looked like thousands of kids and parents moving suitcases and bags, hugging and kissing, and saying goodbye.

"I'm not ready," I announced. "Let's just go back home. Space can wait." I re-fastened my seatbelt and folded my hands in my lap.

My parents looked at me and then at each other with confused expressions.

"Sera, you spent months on your application. You insisted on watching *Keeping up with the Kardashians* for research," Dad said, air quoting the word research.

"Well, it's not like you let me watch it anyway," I muttered.

"That's correct," Dad replied. "No reality television before you turn 13."

I rolled my eyes.

"I don't understand why you would want to throw away this opportunity, Sera," said Mom. "You've worked so hard."

I took a shaky breath and looked at Mom and Dad.

Don't cry, Sera. Don't cry, Sera, I told myself. The thought of Ida made me want to scream. W*hat if there are fifty more Idas in there?*

I was afraid I had no chance in getting a spot on Jeronimo's team.

Then I thought of Newton. He didn't quit trying to figure out the universe. If he had, we wouldn't understand gravity, and I wouldn't be able to take a ride into space on one of Jeronimo Musgrave's Martian missions.

"You're right," I said, nodding my head. "Let's do this." I unhooked my seat belt and opened the van door.

Mom and Dad smiled.

As I got out of the van, I looked down at my feet. One pink flip-flop and one white church shoe. *Hot fudge,* I thought. *I can't even get that right.*

For just a second, my heart fluttered, and I worried I wouldn't make it.

Be like Newton, I told myself. *And Jeronimo.*

One wardrobe malfunction wasn't going to get me down. I took a deep breath and moved into the swarm of chattering, hugging, and kissing people. I wasn't sure where we were supposed to go. I stood on my tiptoes and squinted as hard as I could.

Suddenly I felt a smack from behind. I thought I was going to fall forward.

"Excuse you," said a smooth voice from behind me.

Excuse me? I thought. How dare she! I was simply trying to find my way to check-in and I was almost flattened by a she-beast from behind. *No, she-beast, excuse you!*

I readied myself for a polite yet stern confrontation as I turned around to see my attacker.

I stopped, and my mouth dropped open. It was Ida Hammer, all seven feet of her. Well, maybe she wasn't technically seven feet tall, but she was definitely tall for her age.

"Ida," I stammered, looking skyward toward her head. The sun glinted behind her, temporarily blinding me. I used my hand to shield my eyes.

My vision cleared, and I saw her staring at me with narrowed eyes. Her black hair was slicked into a perfect ponytail that sat atop her perfect head. A pink sundress flowed around her. It looked like gossamer, all fluid and sparkly. She looked like she'd just stepped out of an H&M catalog. I was sure Georgia would have been delighted. I looked down at my mismatched shoes and soccer shorts and immediately felt underdressed.

"And you are?" Ida asked, adjusting the large, leather bag on her shoulder.

"Serafina Sterling," I muttered.

Ida jostled her head and contorted her face. "Doesn't ring a bell. What's your twitter handle?"

I blinked. "I don't have one."

"Do you 'gram?" she spat.

I blinked again. *Does she mean gram staining?*

"Blog?"

More blinking.

"Do you speak? Are you in need of first aid?" she asked.

All I could do was blink.

She stared coldly at me. "Whatevs. Listen, I have to go. Follow me, okay. @HammerDown."

And in a swirl of pink fabric, she was lost in the crowd.

Mom touched my shoulder. "Do you know her?" she asked.

I looked up at Mom and kind of lied. "No."

"She seemed ... nice," Mom said.

Both Dad and I laughed.

"Yes, very nice," Dad said, patting me on the back. "Now, let's find check-in so we can get you all set up."

I smiled at my parents. Then I saw my mom's hair begin to rise slowly around her head. My smile faded.

CHAPTER FOUR

Mom touched the top of her head. "Ow!" she said, wincing. "I got shocked."

She looked at my dad and his hair was standing straight up, too. I quickly felt the top of my head and confirmed that my hair also stood on end. I looked around at the kids and parents in the crowd. Everyone's hair was being pulled mysteriously into the air. People's eyes and mouths gaped open as they looked at what was going on. A faint crackling sizzled among the crowd.

For some reason, there was an excessive amount of static electricity in the air. We were either about to be struck by lighting or ...

"Get ready," a deep voice boomed from the sky, "for the time of your liiiiiiiiife!"

Smoke billowed from the top of the building. Electronic music began to play. A deep, thumping beat scattered across the crowd, punctuated by the sound of beaming lasers and swooshing light sabers.

Everyone began to look up and down, whispering, "Who's that?" and "Where's that coming from?" A few people coughed as the smoke slowly settled on the concrete.

Mom pulled me close to her. "Is this part of the event?"

I shrugged my shoulders.

"Are we going to be electrocuted?" she asked.

"Or abducted by aliens?" Dad asked.

A high-pitched buzzing sound began and increased to a shrill squeal.

We all covered our ears with our hands.

Something large appeared and hovered, blocking out the sun, above the Musgrave Space building. Everyone's faces turned dark as the shadow stretched across the gathered crowd.

"Today is the first day of the rest"—colored lights began to strobe—"of"—the object gently floated toward the ground—"your liiiiiiiiiiiiiiives!"

Between the billowing smoke and the bright, flashing lights, I couldn't make out what was in the sky. I squinted, trying to see.

"Is that an aircraft?" someone cried.

"Is it a spaceship?" asked someone else.

"Mommy, hold me!" another person shouted.

Mom squeezed my shoulder. "I think this is part of it," she said in a shaky voice. "Yes. This has to be part of it."

The dark thing above descended.

"Today," the booming voice said, "is the day you officially become ... "

The thing settled on the ground. Smoke plumed and the music got louder.

"... junior astronauts!"

The lights flickered.

Suddenly, breaking through the smoke, a green mohawk emerged. I knew immediately who it was.

"It's Jeronimo," I whispered.

Jeronimo Musgrave ran into the crowd. His spikey plume of emerald hair glinted in the flashing lights. He started to clap his hands to the beat of the music. "Good morning, space adventurers!" he yelled.

All at once, the crowd broke into hysterics.

"It's him! That's Jeronimo!" a boy screamed.

"He's here! Jeronimo is really here!" a girl hollered.

Jeronimo, wearing a white flight suit complete with space boots and space gloves, began walking through the crowd, greeting parents and kids. He smiled as he pumped parents' hands and gently patted kids on the back.

The crowd kept screaming.

A girl came running toward me. "It's a table," she cried. "He flew the check-in table!"

My parents and I immediately turned our heads toward the smoking craft that Jeronimo had landed in the middle of the crowd. The girl was right. A jet-powered table sat in the middle of the crowd, still crackling and hissing.

The table was like most tables. It had a plastic surface and four metal legs. However, each leg had a fiery corona sparking near the ground.

He must have super-charged the legs, I thought. *That's how he did it. He put little jet engines in the legs.*

A sign, taped to the front of the table, read, "Check In."

I turned to Jeronimo in awe.

"That's amazing!" Dad shouted. Even he was not immune to the charisma of Jeronimo.

Mom laughed. "Don't get any ideas, honey."

Jeronimo came up to my parents. "Good morning, folks," he said. "Thanks for trusting us with your little"—he shuffled some papers he was holding— "Stephanie." He smiled a big, white horse grin.

My parents didn't seem to notice his mistake. They just stood there staring, with weird smirks on their faces. "Yes. Stephanie. Here she is," said Dad.

I stumbled toward Jeronimo as my mother pushed me forward. "Serafina," I managed.

"Huh," he said as he grabbed my hand. "I am so glad you came to my institute. We're going to have a fabulous week."

Before I could say anything else, Jeronimo was gone in a green flash.

"Did he just call me Stephanie?" I asked my parents.

They just smiled their weird, gushy smiles and watched as Jeronimo worked the crowd, pumping hands and patting backs.

"What's that, Stephanie?" Dad asked distractedly.

I rolled my eyes.

CHAPTER FIVE

I sat on the rocket-shaped bed in my room looking at the new phone my parents had given me before they left. I hadn't asked for it. They just handed it to me, out of the blue, in a little, pink gift bag. Dad said I needed it so I could stay in touch. Mom said it was for emergencies only.

I ran my hand across the black, plastic casing.

I was still in shock. I wasn't sure if the shock was because I've been told repeatedly that I was not going to get a phone until I was at least 13 or because my parents had given me a flip phone.

A flip phone! Where do you even find a flip phone? They must have traveled back in time 20 years.

I stared at the ancient artifact. It didn't have a camera or apps or the Internet. It couldn't download Twitter, and I was pretty sure it wouldn't Snapchatter or whatever Georgia called it. It could barely text.

I looked at the analog screen and the words that scrolled across it: *We Love You, Serafina! Mom and Dad.* As I read the words, I felt a giant stab of guilt in my chest. My folks had just given me a great gift, and I'd managed to find something to nit-pick about. Even if it belonged in a museum, I was glad to have a communication device that didn't require stringing together two soup cans.

"Oh, gosh. That sure is nice. My grandma has one just like it," said my roommate, Taffy Carbunkle, pointing toward my phone.

I smiled peevishly. "I guess I'm in good company, then." I slipped the phone into my pocket.

"You betcha! All my folks gave me was this bath set." Taffy held up a basket full of lotions, bubble bath, and fancy gels.

I squinted at the label. "Bacon and sour cream?" I asked. I peered at the dark pink liquid in the bottles.

Taffy shook her head. "Don't ask. My dad says this is proof hipsters are taking over the world." Taffy was from Minnesota and wore her hair in a braid that circled her entire head and looked like that fancy bread you see in the bakery section of the grocery store. When she smiled her cheeks looked like bright pink baby fists and her eyes disappeared. It was like she smiled with her whole face not just her lips.

"So," Taffy said in a conspiratorial whisper, "I know everyone brought gummy worms and Oreos and stuff like that, but, by golly, I have some of the best contraband you'll find here."

She dug around in her bag and brought out a casserole dish.

"What is it?" I asked.

"Hot dish! Dontcha know?" she said with giddy glee. "It's a casserole made with tater tots. My mom made it this morning. Now we won't go hungry. I heard that Jeronimo won't eat anything that had a face. I don't know about you, but I can't live on lettuce."

"We don't have a refrigerator. How are you going to keep it from going bad?"

Taffy pulled out a second container. It was cylindrical and made of metal. "Don't worry. I brought my liquid nitrogen. I never leave home without it. I'm just crazy about material science." Taffy smiled and her eyes once again disappeared.

I grinned as Taffy opened the liquid nitrogen and smoke billowed around her face.

The smoke was all long and gray and stringy making me think of Newton's hair, which made me think of his second law—the law that states that the acceleration of an object is directly proportional to the force that is acting upon it. In other words, it takes more force to move a bigger and heavier object and less to move a smaller, lighter one. It's kind of like pushing someone on a swing. It's really easy to push the smaller, lighter, younger kids at the playground, but it's really hard to push the bigger, older kids.

Thinking about Newtonian force and the energy required to move something heavy made me think of Ida. That's a lot of energy.

If I wanted to win a spot on Jeronimo's team, I was going to have to muster up all the force I had to try and move Ida Hammer out of my way. Especially now that I knew the real Jeronimo, the Jeronimo who liked to attach jet engines to check-in tables and fly into his institute. He was a super flashy, super genius, super important guy. I was just Serafina Marina Sterling, and I had a hard time remembering to wear a matching pair of shoes in the morning.

Taffy seemed to read my mind. "Are you wearing those to the opening ceremony?" she asked, pointing at my mismatched shoes with a polite smiled plastered on her face.

I shrugged. "Sure."

"Good for you," she said, putting her arm over my shoulder. "I like you, Serafina. You aren't afraid to be you. We're going to have a great time together."

Taffy and I left our room and followed a line of giggling and whispering kids into the auditorium.

"Wow!" Taffy and I said as we arrived in the Musgrave auditorium. We stopped and spun slowly with our heads in the air.

The entire place was lit up with stars. It was like standing in the middle of the solar system. On the ceiling, the northern hemisphere slowly rotated. Orion and the dippers stood out prominently amongst the sparkling constellations. The walls blazed brightly with twinkling points of pink, blue, green, yellow, and orange lights, flashing to an unheard rhythm. My head swam, and my heart started to beat rapidly.

As I spun, I found myself, once again, stumbling into someone. I swung around expecting to see Ida. Instead, it was a girl with long, black hair draped over her shoulders like a curtain. She was wrapped in a bright pink sari.

"Excuse me," she said, touching my arms gently. "I

didn't mean to run into you. I was captivated by these stars and wasn't paying attention." She motioned toward the ceiling.

"I'm sorry," I said, rubbing my head in embarrassment. "I was doing the same thing."

"I'm Padma." She extended her hand for a friendly handshake. "And this is my friend Emmanuel." She pointed toward a boy wearing something that looked like a bright orange dress. It was festooned with green and yellow geometric patterns. Underneath the dress, he wore pants of the same pattern.

"I'm Serafina, and this is my roommate, Taffy."

"Very nice to meet you folks," Taffy said. "I hope you like hugs."

Padma and Emmanuel smiled as Taffy squeezed them in giant bear hugs.

"So where are you guys from?" I asked.

"Emmanuel is from Lagos," said Padma, "and I am from Hyderabad."

Taffy looked at me with confusion. I guess she had never heard of those places before either.

"Is that in Texas?" I asked.

"No," Emmanuel said, with a little chuckle.

"California?" Taffy asked.

"No, silly," Padma said. "Lagos is a town in Nigeria, and Hyderabad is in India."

"You guys are from totally different countries?" I asked.

"For cryin' out loud!" Taffy shouted and slapped her thighs. "We've got people from all over the world here."

Padma giggled. "Yes. We are from different countries. I met Emmanuel at check-in."

"I thought your accents were kind of funny," Taffy said.

Padma and Emmanuel giggled.

"We thought yours were funny, too," Padma said, cupping her hand over her mouth as she continued to laugh.

We all giggled and looked at the stars.

"Can I ask you something, Emmanuel?" I said after a few moments.

"Sure."

"Is that a dress you're wearing? I mean I hope I'm not offending you. I'm just curious." I felt my face flush hot at the question.

Emmanuel smiled. "No worries, Serafina. I'm glad you asked. This is a traditional garment for men in my country. It's called an agbada."

I nodded my head. "It's really nice. I've never seen anything like it."

In fact, there were a lot of things I had never seen. I looked around the crowd at all the different faces and hair and clothes. My head began to swim again, and Newton's second law popped back into my mind. I was going to need a lot of force to be able to move my way onto Jeronimo's junior astronaut team. The competition was going to be fierce.

As if she could smell my fear, Ida Hammer—all seven feet of her—appeared from behind Padma. She wore a totally different outfit from earlier. Somehow, this one made her seem even older and scarier. She wore black, skinny jeans with high-heeled boots and a shirt that read "#winner" in bold lettering. She looked like one of the lady villains from my dad's old James Bond movies.

She raised one perfectly arched brow and split our group as she proceeded forward. At least five other kids trailed behind her.

"Is that Ida Hammer?" Taffy asked, her mouth hanging open.

I nodded my head slowly.

"I heard she knows 13 languages," Padma said.

"I heard she was short listed for the Nobel," Emmanuel said.

"I heard she's getting her own reality show," Taffy said.

"Why is she even competing?" I asked feeling frustrated. "There's no way we can win against someone like her."

Everyone fell silent for a moment.

"We all have an equal chance," Taffy said with an upbeat tone.

"Sure we do," Padma said.

We all fell silent again and watched as Ida moved deftly through the crowd of space adventurers. Kids everywhere spun their heads upward to look as she walked through the auditorium. Everyone must have known who she was.

"Are you ladies ready for the original invention presentation?" Emmanuel asked, changing the topic.

I shrugged my shoulders. "When is that again?"

"What!" shouted Taffy, Padma, and Emmanuel all

at once.

I stiffened in shock. "What, what?" I asked.

"What, what?" Taffy said. "Tonight is the presentation, Serafina." She pointed to her watch. "Like in 15 minutes."

I felt my belly turn to a hot, quivering liquid. "Fifteen minutes?"

"Fifteen minutes!" Padma repeated.

"Fifteen minutes," Emmanuel chided.

"My invention is in the room! What am I going to do? I thought I was going to have at least one night to rehearse my speech!"

My brain was starting to misfire. I was in full-on, freak-out mode! I had been so wrapped up in worrying about Ida that I had forgotten to look at the schedule. Big mistake!

Taffy grabbed both of my shoulders. "Run!" she yelled.

I turned back toward the dorms and began to sprint.

"Wait! Not yet!" she yelled with her hand cupped over her mouth. "Come back."

"Okay," I said in a breathless whisper and ran back toward the group.

"You need a plan," Padma said.

I nodded my head.

"We are going to save you a seat while you go get your invention ready," Taffy said as she pulled out her schedule. "It looks like you should have 30 minutes to get your invention ready, practice your speech a few times, and get it together for pete's sake! Can you do that?"

I nodded my head vigorously.

"Then go. Run, Serafina! Run!"

CHAPTER SIX

I fell, gasping and panting, into my seat exactly 28 minutes later.

"Did I miss it?" I asked Taffy. "My presentation?"

"No," she whispered. "But hush! Look!" She pointed to the stage.

It was Ida. It must have been her turn to take the stage. At some point between entering the auditorium and her presentation she'd changed into a gold lamé space suit trimmed in western-style fringe. She waltzed up to the stage like a rock star, wearing a hands-free mic, and looking like a cross between Buzz Aldrin and Ke$ha.

Ida stood at center stage and raised her arms into a V. It was like she was summoning her minions, a move only Beyoncé and dictators of small communist countries could pull off. This simple motion whipped the crowd into a frenzy. People leapt to their feet, hooting and hollering. Fireworks shot into the air and laser lights began dancing around her. A glitter bomb rained golden sparkles down on our heads. Jeronimo, who had been sitting quietly in a chair on the corner of the stage, began to clap and stomp his feet to the rhythm of Ida's deep bass music.

"This is amazeballs!" Ida shouted to her adoring fans. "Totes amazeballs!" She lifted her head toward the glitter spray and spun with the grace of a ballerina. As she circled back toward the crowd we could see something in her hand.

"Is that her invention?" Padma asked.

"But it's so teeny meeny," Taffy replied.

"I can't see anything," I moaned. "I think that glitter scratched my corneas."

"Shhhh," Taffy chided. "I need to see this."

"Is that ... Is that ..." Emmanuel peered hard at the stage.

"A fidget spinner?" Emmanuel, Padma and Taffy said all at one time.

Through some brilliant engineering and use of gyroscopes, Ida had created a zero-gravity fidget spinner that was completely encrusted in Swarovski crystals! As she unveiled her device and began to spin it in her hands, the crowd roared with glee.

"Space travel can be totes boring," said Ida, spinning her device as she walked back and forth across the stage. "Now, with my zero-gravity Hammerizer, you will never be bored. The Hammerizer utilizes the most advanced technology thanks to my patented micro-gyroscopes, and it's also super relevant. Your fellow astronauts will be hindered by gravity and their lame taste in fidget spinners that are, like, so yesterday, while you will be the most with my crystal-encrusted, zero-gravity Hammerizer."

"Go ahead," she added. "Check under your chairs. There's one for everybody."

Everyone looked. Sure enough, Ida had placed Hammerizers underneath each chair. They all were encrusted with crystals and had the words "#HammerDown" written on the front. Kids screamed and cheered as they picked up their very own crystal-encrusted spinner.

Taffy shrieked. "My mom won't even let me have an ordinary fidget spinner! Now, look! Look at me, Serafina! I'm fidgeting! And spinning!"

Ida paced back and forth on the stage while she spun her Hammerizer over and over to the shrieks of the crowd.

"Spin!" Ida cheered. "Spin! This bad boy doesn't even care about gravity!"

Even Jeronimo had a spinner—one covered in bright green crystals, the same color as his hair.

"Serafina!" Taffy exclaimed. "Where's your phone? I need you to take a picture of me spinning!" Her face fell as remembered that my phone was, as Ida would say, like, so yesterday. "Oh. That's right. It doesn't take pictures." She brightened. "Oh, well! I'm spinning!"

Emmanuel and Padma grinned from ear to ear as they, too, spun their Hammerizers.

"Next up, Stephanie Sterling!" said Jeronimo from the stage.

I groaned.

It was obvious that no one could ever, ever, ever in a million light years, compete with Ida Hammer.

Especially not me. Ida had combined science and awesomeness into one hand-held device.

By the time I went on stage, the crowd had more or less calmed down. The kids who could be classified as "more calm" were too busy spinning their devices in their hands to pay attention. And the kids who could be classified as "less calm" talked to the people next to them, undoubtedly about the amazing show they had just seen.

"Ahem," I cleared my voice into the microphone. I looked down at my mismatched shoes and thought about Ida's glamorous space suit. I squeezed my eyes shut in regret. I wish I had prepared more or at least put on matching shoes!

The crowd continued to spin and chatter. No one even noticed I was at the podium.

I looked at Jeronimo. He sat in the corner of the stage, still spinning his Hammerizer. Green flashes glinted from his spinner as it spun.

"Ahem," I tried again, feeling my throat grow scratchy and dry. "Ahem!"

"Kaboom!" An explosion erupted behind me.

I covered my head and curled into a ball as I hid for cover beneath the podium. The crowd gasped and screamed.

That must have been a pyrotechnic that had misfired during Ida's presentation, I thought. *I should be safe now*, I reasoned.

I slowly stood and took my place back at the podium, gripping the sides with my sweaty palms.

The crowd grew silent. Hammerizers slowly ceased

spinning. Gradually, everyone's eyes moved toward me.

I took a deep breath and swallowed. I pressed both of my hands into my quivering belly, as Newton's third law raced through my mind.

Newton's third law states that for every action there is an equal and opposite reaction. It's the reason we can go to space—the action of the combustion engine creates a force that acts upon the ground, which generates the reaction of the rocket lifting into the air and eventually into space. It's way symmetrical; when any force acts upon an object like the combustion engine of the rocket acting upon the ground, an equal yet opposite reaction occurs like the rocket lifting into space. Tit for tat. Quid pro quo. An eye for an eye. Scientifically speaking, of course.

This was Newton's third law working in a way that I had never expected. Ida's presentation was the action, and my presentation was the reaction. While Ida shined and sparkled with her beautiful outfit and amazing pyrotechnics, I stood on stage silent and scared, in my brother's old basketball jersey, reacting. Ida was the hammer, and I was the nail. She stood tall while I was being flattened.

Here's goes nothing, I thought.

"Soooo. I'm supposed to be presenting my invention," I said, and the microphone squealed.

Kids winced in the crowd and covered their ears from the obnoxious noise.

"Sorry. Sorry about that," I adjusted the mic. "Yep. Yeah. That should do it."

A lone cough echoed in the auditorium.

I looked into the crowd and saw Taffy giving me the double thumbs up.

I smiled.

"I'm here to present my invention."

More coughing in the crowd.

"It's a hugging machine," I said.

A sharp laugh came from the back of the auditorium.

I jerked my head up to see who laughed. I squinted, but it was too dark to make out any faces.

"Like I was saying,"—I pulled the machine from my backpack and attached a diode to each of my elbows and hung a necklace around my neck—"I created a hugging machine."

Laughter started again from the back of the auditorium. This time it was louder.

"A hugging machine?" someone asked in a sarcastic tone of voice.

I squinted and held my hand over my eyes, but I still couldn't see who was heckling me.

I took a deep breath and tried to ignore it.

"A mission to Mars is estimated to take months and maybe even years to complete," I explained. "During that time, an astronaut may become homesick. That much time away from everything a person knows and loves may have serious psychological implications."

"We need technology, not therapy. We're astronauts for crying out loud!" Someone yelled from the back of the auditorium.

"Who said that?" I exclaimed.

Giggles began to break out amongst the kids.

"Kids, please," Jeronimo said from his seat. "Let's allow"—he paused to look at a sheet of paper in front of him—"Stephanie to speak."

"Serafina," I said quietly.

"What's that, Stephanie?" Jeronimo asked, cupping one hand over his ear.

"Never mind," I took a ragged breath. "As I was saying, these feelings of loneliness would be detrimental to the mission as it would be very difficult to focus on important tasks like navigation or being an ambassador to undiscovered intelligent life forms. Therefore, I created a technology that would act as a two-way communication device."

"Spaceships already have radios!" a voice yelled from the crowd.

The giggles got louder, but Jeronimo didn't seem to notice. He just sat there spinning his Hammerizer.

My eyes felt kind of stingy, like they were being blasted with sand. I blinked.

"The way this works is that someone on Earth will wear this device and so will you. You will have a necklace"—I pointed to the necklace around my neck—"and so will your loved one on Earth, like your mom or dad or maybe even your best friend. You'll also have these diodes" —I pointed to my elbows— "and so will your loved one. When you start to feel a little lonely from millions and millions of miles of space travel, you simply hug yourself, like this." I demonstrated a self-hug by grabbing both of my elbows and squeezing. The heart-shaped charm on the necklace lit up. "When you hug yourself, the necklace on Earth will light up, indicating that a hug is taking place."

The entire crowd began to laugh.

My eyes started to sting more, and I blinked rapidly. I cleared my throat again. "It works the same for your loved one. When your necklace lights up, you know you are getting a hug all the way from Earth."

More laughter.

I blinked my eyes more because the stinging was getting worse. This time, to my horror, a tear slid out. I quickly wiped it and continued. "It's kind of like a hug radio."

"Someone needs a hug," the voice jeered.

The crowd erupted in laughter.

I looked out at their faces in horror. Kids were doubling over, pointing and laughing at me.

Tears began to fall from my eyes like a dripping faucet.

I scanned the laughing faces to find my friends. Padma, Emmanuel, and Taffy's faces were bright red. I could tell they were embarrassed as well. I wondered if they were embarrassed because they knew me.

"Simmer down," Jeronimo said casually. "Simmer down." He rose to his feet. "Stephanie. Thank you for your presentation. You can take your seat now." He motioned toward the stairs. He wasn't pumping his fist or cheering for me.

As I ran off the stage, I turned my head toward the crowd.

Ida stood up with her hand cupped around her mouth. "Hugging machines are super basic!" she shouted.

It was Ida the entire time. She was the one yelling from the back of the crowd.

"Look! Her shoes don't even match! How basic!" Ida shouted as the laughter from the auditorium rose like a licking flame.

"Basic people need hugs, too! Someone give this basic girl a hug!" she bellowed.

The entire group was now snickering and laughing at me.

I had just been whacked by Ida the Hammer.

Georgia was right. I was a weirdo, a freak, a geek. Ida had declared it to the entire group. Georgia also was correct in predicting Ida's bloodthirsty nature. Now Georgia could add doomsday prophet to her resume right after super-freakishly organized. I'd be sure to let her know once I got home. If I made it home.

CHAPTER SEVEN

That night, as I lay in my rocket-shaped bed, tossing and turning, I felt the sting of Newton and his third law. The law that states for every action there is an equal and opposite reaction.

I had been labeled a "basic girl" at Musgrave Space Adventure. I wasn't even sure what that meant, but even I, Serafina Sterling, the queen of no fashion or style and proud owner of a brand new flip phone, knew that being labeled a freak amongst pre-teen science enthusiasts was hard to do. These were the same people who did recreational chemistry and enjoyed calculus—definitely not "normal" kid stuff. And when you are not normal in your everyday life it sure is nice to find a place where you fit in. Like a space adventure. Except, not me. Thanks to Ida, I didn't fit in anywhere, even at a space adventure. It seemed I would be the freak among geeks.

The next morning was even worse.

My friends and I sat quietly around our breakfast trays, trying, I guessed, to forget my presentation ever happened. At least, I knew I was. As we picked at our food, Ida's voice traveled cross the cafeteria.

"Guys, I'm totes eating clean this week," Ida moaned toward the frustrated looking cafeteria workers.

"And what exactly do you think this food is? Dirty?" a lady in a white apron asked Ida.

Ida shook her head. "No, no, no. Clean. Clean eating. As in dairy free, gluten free, pesticide free. Don't you have anything organic? Grass fed? Non-GMO? Free range?"

"Kid, the only thing we have that's free range is those grapes that escaped from the buffet line." The server pointed toward some grapes that were slowly rolling across the floor.

"Whatevs." Ida stuck a large donut in her mouth and snatched up her tray. "Where's the espresso machine?" she yelled aloud.

I looked toward my friends. "Why is she is such a bad mood?" I asked. "She has nothing to be upset about."

Emmanuel nodded his head slowly.

"I'm the one who should be upset," I said.

Taffy huffed. "I just don't understand why she had to be so ugly. I mean hot tomatoes, she was so stinkin' mean I could just ..." She sighed in exasperation before even finishing her sentence.

Taffy, Padma, and Emmanuel all gave me the same sympathetic look they had given me one million times since last night. Sympathy made me crazy, and my friends were feeling pretty sorry for me. Of course they had good reason. I totally, utterly, hopelessly, flamboyantly bombed my original invention presentation.

Everyone's back stiffened as Ida walked near our table. All at once, my friends seemed much more interested in their trays than they did at having a conversation.

Ida must have sensed our weakness, like a shark smelling blood in the water, because her mood seemed to immediately improve.

She smiled at the table as she swung a donut around her finger. "This is so awks. No one's talking. What's the matter, Serafina? Do you need a hug?" She began to cackle wildly in her super-evil lady villain laugh.

Taffy sneered. "Why don't you just leave her alone, Ida? You've done enough, dontcha know?"

Ida raised one perfect eyebrow. "YOLO," she said as she walked away.

Ida's words stung. It was a stinging that began last night and hadn't stopped yet.

The original invention presentation was intense. Not only had I totally goofed on when I thought the actual presentation was going to be, I had completely underestimated the amazing, original, and completely innovative inventions the other kids had created.

I had just wanted to create a device to ease the pain of space travel. I knew flying between planets was way more difficult than the three-hour road trip my family and I took once a month to Granny Mary's house, and that was hard enough with my baby brother Horton's smelly diaper and holding your tinkle until Dad could find a clean bathroom. The moon is about 250,000 miles away and it usually takes about a week to fly there and back. Any normal person could live off weird food for a week, but Mars is over 255 million miles away! That's like nine months of travel, and that's only one way!

It was hard to imagine being in the same old space ship for nine months, but I knew there was something I'd miss more than good food and clean water. I knew I would miss my family and my friends. I might even miss Apollo and his gigantic smelly feet! So when it came to inventing, I created something that would make me near the people I cared about most, even when I was 255 million miles away.

I had thought it was a great invention. But now, after last night's horrible presentation and the dull looks on my friends' faces, I knew I'd made a mistake. I was toast. No way was I getting into the astronaut program now, especially with Ida the Hammer intent on destroying me.

CHAPTER EIGHT

"Aunt Celeste," I said into my flip phone the next morning. "Do you have a minute?"

"Serafina?" she said. "What's the matter? I sense negativity. It's something about your energy. It's off. Have you been smudging? You need to smudge. How are your chakras? Are you using those crystals I gave you at Christmas?"

I shook my head. "No, no, Aunt Celeste. I don't need to smudge. And I don't even remember where my chakra is. Is that the goopy looking thing at the back of my throat?"

"No? Then what is it, my dear sunflower? Why are you calling with such dread in your voice?"

I could hear muffled conversation in the background and something that sounded like a drum.

"Where are you?" I asked, nervously chewing on my fingernails

"Sedona, my little milkweed. Arizona! It's fabulous, simply fabulous. I'm doing a vision quest."

"Vision quest?" I asked. "Are you looking for something?"

"We're all looking for something, my little dew drop. But yes, I am looking for the meaning of life."

I blinked. "Well, let me know what you find out."

I stood up and began to nervously pace in my room. Taffy was gone. She was in Padma's dorm preparing for this morning's activity: a ride on the vomit comet. We'd had an early wake-up call, and I wasn't feeling quite right. I was tired and anxious and feeling completely overwhelmed. I needed to talk—and not to my parents.

I didn't want them to worry about me, but more importantly I didn't want them to know how awfully, terribly this space adventure was going. Both my folks had spent hours and hours helping me prepare my application, and they'd shown me constant encouragement and support. They had even gotten me a phone! Even though it wasn't a cool, shiny iPhone like the one Georgia had, they'd still broken their own oppressive rule about technology.

"I need to talk to you," I said in a whispered tone.

"Enough with the drums, Tony!" Aunt Celeste shouted at someone in a deep, scary tone like she was an old-timey mobster from one of those movies my dad loved so much. Suddenly the beating stopped. Aunt Celeste cleared her throat, and her voice returned to normal, "Go ahead, my tiny bluebonnet. Anything you need."

I took a deep breath. "How do you make someone not hate you?" I pushed out all the words I had wanted to say as fast as I could possibly manage. It felt good to get it all out. It felt even better to ask for some advice.

There was silence on the other end of the line.

"Who hates you, Serafina?" Aunt Celeste asked with obvious concern.

I closed my eyes and pictured Ida in the back of the auditorium, laughing and shouting as I presented my hugging machine.

"It's not important," I said.

"But it is," my aunt replied. "I'm concerned. Are you okay?"

I was silent for a few beats. "I'm okay. I'm just ... sad, I guess."

Aunt Celeste gasped on the other end of the line. "My sweet little peony. That breaks my heart." She cleared her throat and her scary, mobster voice returned. "Who is it? Who is making you sad? You let me know and I'll take care of those dirty, rotten ..."

"Aunt Celeste!" I cried.

She cleared her throat again. "What I mean," she said, as her breathy, yoga voice came back, "what I mean is that I don't want to see you sad."

I smiled at her words. "Thanks."

Even though I couldn't see her because my super-obsolete flip phone couldn't Facetime or Skype or anything like that, I knew she was smiling, too.

"I don't know exactly why someone would hate my darling little daisy, but I do have some experience in this area," she said.

"You do?" I asked.

"Of course, my little buttercup. You know, not everyone thinks I'm as cool as you think I am."

My eyes grew wide. While I did love my aunt Celeste, wearing floor-length tunics and asking strangers to meditate with you didn't usually make you all that cool. "Really?" I asked in what sounded like a total phony voice.

"No," she said enthusiastically. "People hardly ever appreciate the true Celeste. Just the other day someone called me a smelly hippie. Can you believe that?"

"No," I said again in my really fake voice. Just this once, I was glad I couldn't Facetime. I hadn't quite perfected my super-fake, super-plastered-on smile. Georgia says that smile makes me look like Frankenstein's monster after a double espresso.

"It's true!" she shouted. "I was just as shocked as you are."

I smiled again, but this time for real.

"So I do have your answer—" Aunt Celeste began.

"Serafina!" The door flew open, and Taffy's voice echoed around the room. "Come on! It's about to start, dontcha know?"

I turned frantically to see Taffy, Padma, and Emmanuel all smiling at the door.

Taffy motioned toward the hallway. "Hurry up! We can't be late."

"I gotta go," I said sharply into the phone.

"But I have your answer ..."

Those were the last words I heard right before I snapped the phone shut.

CHAPTER NINE

Jeronimo stood in front of the group, the morning sun glinting through his green mohawk. "Today we will be taking a ride on the vomit comet," he shouted through his megaphone. "So I hope that everyone complied with our fasting rules."

Emmanuel, Taffy, and Padma all gave each other worried looks.

"The vomit comet?" Padma repeated, putting her hands on her belly. "I totally forgot that was today!"

"When were we supposed to stop eating?" Emmanuel asked.

"Eight p.m.," I replied.

"That's not good," Taffy said. "You and I finished the last of the hot dish at 10 o'clock!"

"Hot dish?" Padma asked.

"It's a casserole with tater tots," I said.

Padma cocked her head. "Tater tots?"

"Nevermind," I replied. "We can't be the only ones who broke the fasting rules."

Emmanuel shook his head. "My roommate and I ate two pounds of gummy sharks just this morning."

Padma's eyes grew wide. "I ate an entire box of Girl Scout cookies last night."

"If excessive vomiting occurs during flight, you will be asked to leave the plane," Jeronimo said through the megaphone. "Please remember the rules that you had signed *and* notarized."

The vomit comet technically was not a comet. It was actually a "reduced gravity aircraft" meaning it was a plane that could produce zero gravity on Earth. It was used to train future astronauts.

One of the major things that astronauts have to get used to is the feeling of weightlessness. That is generally a very hard thing to attain here on Earth, what with our super-stable gravity and all. So in order to simulate weightlessness, NASA began to take large planes on parabolic flights.

What that means is that an aircraft, a KC-135A, flies in a curving pattern as opposed to its normal, straight-line flight path in order to create the feeling of weightlessness on board. These flights allow astronauts in training a chance to feel what weightlessness is all about. Apparently, it also gives people a chance to revisit their most recent meals because they don't call it the vomit comet for nothing. All that moving up and down in the plane is hard on the belly. Most people blow chunks after just a few dips in the plane.

Taffy waved her hands as if to dismiss Jeronimo's warning. "We're not the only ones with illegal contraband. I heard Ida had six dozen French macarons delivered just last night, dontcha know."

I scrunched my nose. "Don't say her name," I moaned. "I haven't even gone zero gravity, and you're making me feel nauseous."

Taffy tilted her head. "Sorry."

It was day three of the space adventure and things had gone from bad to worse. Since my disastrous presentation of the hugging machine on the first night, I had become the laughing stock of the entire group. Thanks to Ida's heckling, everyone thought me and my invention were super lame, or as Ida said, "basic."

Random kids yelled, "I need a hug" or "Only basic scientists invent hugs!" every time I walked in a room. So far, I had been able to refrain from informing them that their statements were not only rude but also incorrect. Basic scientists investigate empirical disciplines. It was both emotionally and intellectually offensive. But I knew it wouldn't help. Ida was so committed to destroying me that she had shirts made with the phrase "#basicscientistsinventhugmachines" on the front. Apparently, I was trending.

At least none of my new friends had abandoned me. In fact, they were the only reason I hadn't called my parents on my flip phone and asked them to come and take me home. That, and I couldn't bear to let them down.

"They're wearing that darn tootin' shirt," Taffy hissed under her breath.

I looked at a group of girls behind me. They were indeed wearing the shirt Ida had made. It was bright green and the letters were embossed in a glittery gold font.

I rolled my eyes.

"I'm impressed though, dontcha know," Taffy added.

"Why?" Emmanuel, Padma, and I asked at the same time.

Taffy began to wave her hands. "Calm down. Calm down. Not by the shirts, just by the customer service. I mean she had those made and delivered practically overnight. That is a serious commitment to service. We had shirts made for our family reunion and dontcha know it took them almost two months to make it to Minnesota. I'd like to know what provider she used," she said as she tapped her chin.

"Seriously, Taff?" I asked, throwing my hands in the air.

"I'm just sayin'," she replied sheepishly. "Customer service is a dying art."

I saw a seven-foot shadow cast from behind me. I closed my eyes. I knew exactly who it was.

"Yo, Serafina?" Ida asked with her arms extended. "Do you think I could get a hug?" She began to laugh wildly.

"Leave her alone," Padma said. "You've already done enough."

Ida narrowed her eyes at Padma. "Maybe you'd like a hug, too."

"What's wrong with you, Ida? Why can't you just leave Serafina alone?" Padma asked.

"Because," Ida snapped, "this is an institute for astronauts, not basic people with basic brains.

Serafina needs to go back home and hug all her basic friends with her basic hugging machine and leave the space travel to us."

I hung my head and rubbed my eyes. The arteries in my temples pounded loudly enough I could practically hear them.

"What's a matter, baby? Do you need a hug? You're in luck. I hear there is a great machine for that," Ida said, still laughing.

The kids around us started laughing, too. I felt bile rise in my throat.

Before I could say or do anything, my friends grabbed me by the arms and led me away.

"Just ignore her," Padma said.

"She's right," Emmanuel added. "Don't dignify her response with anger or it will make her vicious."

"Vicious?" I moaned. "She had shirts made."

"With some high quality material," Taffy added.

"Taffy!" we all exclaimed.

"Sorry," she said.

"Listen up," Jeronimo barked into his megaphone. "We will be breaking you guys out into groups of five. These groups have been randomly selected by my Musgrave random number generator, trademarked and patent pending."

"I hope I'm not with Ida," I moaned.

"That might be a good thing," Taffy said and smiled. "You have all that wonderful hot dish rolling around in your belly."

My friends snickered.

"Group one!" Jeronimo shouted.

"My stomach feels horrible just looking at those shirts," I said. I scanned the crowd and counted at least 15 kids wearing them.

"Moses Munfree ..."

"Try to take a few deep breaths," Padma said.

"Teddy Pedigrew ..."

"Breathe in, breathe out, " Padma instructed.

"Sara Washington ..."

I sucked in a giant breath and slowly blew it out.

"Ida Hammer ..."

"Nice. Just keep breathing," Padma cooed.

I closed my eyes and took another breath.

"And Stephanie Sterling."

The breath got jammed in my lungs. "What?" I croaked.

I heard Ida's voice shout over the crowd. "Won't you sit next to me, Stephanie? I think I need a hug."

"If you heard your name called, please come forward. We will be boarding in 10 minutes," Jeronimo yelled. "Repeat. Group one will be boarding in 10 minutes."

My friends gave me pathetic little waves as I slunk over to the waiting members of group one.

Jeronimo puzzled over Teddy's shirt. "Hashtag what?" he asked. "Never mind. What I need to know is have you kids been complying to the fasting rule?"

Everyone slowly nodded his or her head in an unconvincing manner.

Jeronimo squinted. "I'm serious, guys. No barfing. I can't take it. I have this thing that if I see someone else barf I immediately get sick." He shuddered like he was imagining barf landing in his lap. "No barfing," he repeated.

We all stood in a silent circle.

"Get your gear on and meet me on the plane," he said as made his way onto the vomit comet.

"Quick, Serafina. I need a hug. Can you hook me up?" Ida asked as the rest of the group laughed at her tired, old joke.

I quickly zipped my flight suit and made my way onto the plane.

"Alright, kids," a tinny voice said over the plane's speakers. "We're just completing a few items from our pre-flight checklist, and then we should be good to go. I hope everyone is ready for some air time!"

"Quick, Serafina. Send me a hug. I'm wearing my necklace. Send it now," Ida mocked, her eyes narrowing.

When Ida said nasty things to me her eyes got all narrow and her nostrils flared big and wide like a cow's.

I rolled my eyes and tried to quiet my belly as the other kids laughed.

"What's that?" Jeronimo asked.

Ida cleared her throat. "Oh nothing, Jeronimo. Stephanie was just a little nervous about the flight so I was trying to comfort her. Maybe this is the first time she's ever flown." She innocently batted her eyes at Jeronimo.

"Stephanie, do you feel like you're going to barf?" Jeronimo asked in his typically clueless way.

For a brilliant genius, Jeronimo sure had proven

himself to be limited in basic social interaction. First of all, he had called me "Stephanie" all week even though I had corrected him like 500 times and was wearing a name tag that clearly stated my name was "S-E-R-A-F-I-N-A." Second, Ida had been torturing me right under his nose and he hadn't even noticed. Not even once! She had half the kids wearing bright green t-shirts that mocked me for goodness sake and he hadn't so much as batted an eyelash.

"Serafina," I said.

Jeronimo gave me a puzzled glance.

"My name?"

Jeronimo looked at me again like I was speaking Egyptian.

The kids began to giggle.

I looked around and felt something new. For three days, I had been feeling angry and raw and just plain mad. Every time I heard Ida say something or hand out another shirt I got all fired up, like a Bunsen burner igniting from within. As I got on that plane, though, I felt something that I didn't expect; it must have been something like surrender.

Suddenly, I felt lonely. Lonely and sad. I had nothing left to give.

CHAPTER TEN

I took a deep breath and found a seat. I settled in for the ride and fastened my lap belt.

"Okay, kids. Buckle up. We will be making our first ascent shortly. After the co-pilot and I have given you the all-clear, you will be able to begin to have some fun in zero gravity," the pilot announced over the loud speaker.

Ida chose a seat directly in front of me, right next to Jeronimo.

Suck up, I thought.

As she fastened her belt, she gave me a sneering glance over her shoulder.

"So, Jeronimo," she began, "how are you liking the Hammerizer?"

I closed my eyes and tried to tune her out as I felt the engines roar to life.

As the plane jostled and moved, I relaxed my head into my seat and began to try and find a happy place in my mind. My brain shuffled though lots of scenarios: star gazing with my best friend, Tori; bug collecting on Tuesday nights; and eating at my favorite place in the entire world, Build-It Burrito. My mind settled on Build-It. A smile curled my lips into a tiny bow, and I licked my lips.

Build-It Burrito was unlike any normal restaurant. It was a place sent straight from heaven. Build-It allowed people to customize their burritos with literally thousands of different ingredients. Thousands! The sheer amount of ingredients in Build-It's offering allowed for infinite flavor combinations. Some of my favorite included the sweet and sour fish sticks, chicken and jelly beans, and bar-b-que pork with queso and curry. A food critic once named Build-It the worst restaurant in America. I took his designation as a badge of honor because he seemed rather sour and could probably benefit from the dreamy taste of a sushi and banana on a spinach tortilla with extra ranch dressing.

I shifted in my seat as my stomach grumbled. *My imagination must be super solid*, I thought, *because I can almost taste the curry in my mouth.*

"This is your pilot speaking. We're almost ready for zero gravity to commence. Make sure all unfastened items are properly stowed. Please remember your training, and most of all please respect your fellow astronauts. Over and out."

I opened my eyes and began to unlatch my lap belt. I touched my belly as my stomach grumbled once more. *I do have a wonderful imagination*, I thought.

Ida was already on her feet and held two Hammerizers in her hand.

"Should you put those away, Ida?" Teddy asked.

"They could get loose once we hit zero gravity and do some damage."

Ida sneered at Teddy. "These are zero-gravity Hammerizers. DUH! Zero gravity. They will just go on spinning in my hand as soon as we hit that zero g."

Teddy blinked a few times. "Sorry."

"Look, Jeronimo," Ida said. "You're going to get to see my invention perform in zero gravity!" She smiled broadly and noticed me looking at her. She grimaced in my direction.

I sighed and felt another pinch in belly.

Jeronimo got to his feet and said, "I never did get to ask you how you were able to test your invention under zero-gravity conditions. Do you have a simulator near your lab?"

Ida began to blink rapidly and pursed her lips into a fine line. "No, no simulator," she responded.

The nose of the plane began to point downward, and I started to feel the first inkling of weightlessness. It began in my toes. It was like my feet were being pushed from the ground. I smiled and thought to myself, *Newton, you manly beehive wearer, you sure know what you're doing!* This was the way I liked to think of my Newtonian laws, working in my favor for once.

"Weeeeee!" I said and raised my hands over my head as I began to take flight. It was the most amazing feeling I had ever had!

Everyone else began to slowly lift from the ground as well.

"Whoa!" Moses yelled.

"Yeehaw!" Sara screamed.

Jeronimo, undoubtedly used to being in zero-gravity situations, continued speaking as he took flight. "Then how exactly do you know these spinners will remain functional under zero-gravity conditions?" he asked.

Ida began to look nervous. "Well. Theory, I suppose." She shrugged her shoulders.

Just as she said that the two Hammerizers began to take flight across the cabin.

"Watch out!" I yelled. "They aren't meant for zero gravity! They're just regular fidget spinners!"

The two Hammerizers began to dart wildly and dangerously across the cabin as we soared higher and higher in the air.

Everyone, including Jeronimo, buried their head in their arms.

"How can you say it's 'zero gravity' if you didn't test it?" he yelled.

Just then, one of the Hammerizers hit me in my belly. Then something strange started to happen.

As the Hammerizer punched my gut, my brain began flashing images of food. Somehow, the Hammerizer had flipped an internal switch. It was like I had a mini-movie screen right behind my eyes. I began to see pictures of gummy sharks and hot dish and curry-noodle burritos and pink French macarons in high definition. As these pictures flashed, a vibration began somewhere in the vicinity of my toes. This vibration was slow and barely noticeable at first. As it grew stronger, the wave slowly rose up my legs, through my butt, and into my pinchy belly.

"Ohhhhhh," I groaned as I held my tummy. "I don't feel so good."

Jeronimo's eyes grew wide. "Oh no. Oh no!" he yelled.

I felt a tidal wave somewhere down deep. Before I knew it, I felt a splashing wave of contraband hot dish casserole come rushing forth. "BLEEEUUUUUURRRRGGGHHHH!"

Ida, who had been darting around the cabin trying to catch her non-zero-gravity fidget spinners, (which actually made them regular fidget spinners with a bunch of rhinestones) floated gracefully into my stream of puke.

"Ahhh!!!!!" she yelled as a goopy tater tot nailed her in the head.

Another tidal wave came out; this time it nailed Ida on the top of her head.

"AAAACCCCCCKKKKKKK!"

"My hair!" she screamed.

All of a sudden, I heard another familiar grumbling. This time it was Teddy. A stream of pink barf came from her mouth and hit the other side of Ida's head. "PUUUUUUFFFFFFTTTTTTT!"

She must have been eating French macarons with Ida, I thought.

"OH. EM. GEE!" Ida yelled.

It was Jeronimo's turn. He held his hand over his mouth and made weird convulsing moves mid-air. Then a stream ejected from him. "UUUUUGGGGHHHHHH!"

Ida got nailed again, this time in the back. She tried to move away from the streams of puke but couldn't get any traction, what with there being no gravity and all.

Soon the dominos began to fall. After Jeronimo, Sara succumbed, then Moses, and finally Ida.

"Mayday! Mayday!" yelled the pilots from the cockpit, and then they barfed.

CHAPTER ELEVEN

"Mom," I said into the phone in a shaky voice.

"What's the matter, Serafina? Do you have diarrhea? Tell me it isn't diarrhea!" She sounded panicked.

I'm not sure why my mom's mind always went to injury or illness anytime I spoke to her, but it did. One time, I called her from school because I had forgotten my lunch and before I could even ask her anything she was nearly crying because she thought I might have contracted Ebola.

"No, Mom. It's not diarrhea. I just need to tell you and Dad something."

"Oh good. I'm just worried about dehydration, and I know how you love to eat all that greasy food, so I just thought that maybe …"

"Mom! It's not diarrhea!" I shouted.

"Okay, okay!" she said.

"Mom, I'm not sure how to tell you this so I am just going to spit it out …"

She was silent, but in that judgy kind of way that only moms can be silent.

"I'm in trouble," I said finally.

In my 11 years on this cruel, cruel Earth, I had had to deliver many bad pieces of information to my parents. There was that one time when I was experimenting with industrial adhesives and accidently but permanently fused the patio furniture to the back deck. (In my defense, I had been trying to prevent unnecessary trip hazards through the wonder of cyanoacralates.) I'd had to fess up when Dad asked me to pull the chairs under the awning, and I couldn't get them to budge.

Then, there was the time I turned Apollo blue by accidently exposing him to excess silver dust. He'd started freaking out, convinced he was going to look like that giant blueberry girl from *Charlie and the Chocolate Factory* in his profile pic. Mom made me tell her the truth after she heard all of his screaming and crying. On a positive note, I now know argyria (turning blue from excess silver exposure) is neither fatal nor permanent. I can even spell it! But nothing had been as painful as telling my parents that I had gotten into trouble at the Musgrave Space Adventure.

After I told her, she grew even quieter, and not in a good way. Not in the way parents get quiet when they are hiding an awesome secret like an unplanned trip to Mr. Magali's Pizza or when you finally get to go to Disneyland. This was a quiet that made my stomach rumble again.

She handed the phone over to Dad.

"I'm shocked and disappointed, girl squirrel," Dad said. "You broke the rules. But we'll talk later. We're on our way now for the awards ceremony."

"I guess I forgot about the awards," I said to myself under my barfy breath.

I quickly remembered. That night, Jeronimo was going to announce the winner of the original space invention contest. It seemed unlikely that I would be winning anything.

"See you soon," I whispered and gently flipped my phone closed.

Taffy rubbed my shoulder. "Are they mad?" she asked in a low voice.

I shook my head. "Worse."

Taffy nodded her head knowingly. "Disappointed?"

I nodded my head solemnly.

I looked at Padma and Emmanuel who were pretending to flip through books, acting like they weren't interested in my conversation. Emmanuel was holding Taffy's copy of *A Girl's Guide to Facial Glitter*.

"Thinking of updating your look?" I asked Emmanuel, raising my eyebrows and gesturing toward the book.

He looked at the cover. He shook his head and tossed the book onto the bed. "So what's going to happen, Serafina? What kind of trouble are you in?"

I wasn't sure, but I knew it was big. Following the regretful barfing incident on the vomit comet, I had been interrogated by a few of the instructors on whether or not I had violated policy by possessing and consuming illegal contraband items such as the hot dish I blew all over Ida's perfect face. Apparently, the whole thing about Jeronimo really hating vomit was a serious issue. After landing, Jeronimo had laid on the ground in the fetal position, repeating over and over, "The germs won't eat my brains. The germs won't eat my brains." I was told being scared of germs was pretty common among geniuses, but it didn't make it any less weird.

The good news (if anything could be considered good news) was that—while I knew I was in trouble for violating the rules I'd signed and had witnessed by a notary public at the Kinko's down the street from my house—Ida also was in trouble, along with about 10 other kids who (after a raid led by snack-sniffing dogs) were found to be in possession of such items as flaming-hot Cheetos, sour worms, and Swedish fish.

I secretly delighted in the fact that Ida was in trouble because I totally blamed her for making me barf in the first place. All of her bullying and heckling and relentless teasing is what made me feel all woozy and horrible. It stood to reason that I would have never, ever, ever blown chunks in the first place if Ida Hammer had never cast her super-evil shadow on me.

There was a rapid knock on the door. We all grew silent.

Taffy slowly opened the door.

One of the instructors, Ms. Razzy, poked her head through the door. "Serafina? Jeronimo needs to speak with you in his office. Can you come with me, please?"

I slowly rose to my feet and felt my stomach knot

up once again.

I followed Ms. Razzy down a series of winding halls. On the walls, there were about a thousand framed photos of Jeronimo, documenting his lifetime of success. I passed a black and white of him accepting a medal. He must have been in middle school, just like me, because he didn't have a mohawk, and he was sporting a mouth full of metal with bonus headgear. I winced. I saw another photograph of him in a cap and gown crossing a stage, probably receiving one of the three doctoral degrees he earned. There also was a photo of him standing in front of a sign that read "Los Alamos," and another in front of one of his jet cars.

I began to feel saggy and ashamed as I walked by the photographic evidence of his greatness. I didn't see one picture of him barfing on any of his heroes.

Ms. Razzy pointed to a line of chairs in front of Jeronimo's office. Guilty kids filled all but the one—the one next to Ida.

I chose to stand.

"Stephanie," Jeronimo said as he opened his door. He wore gloves and looked as though he had broken out into hives. There were red bumps on his neck and some running up and down his arms.

"Yes," I replied quickly.

He motioned toward his desk, and I made my way into his office.

The inside of his office was seriously amazing. Machines and contraptions of all shapes and sizes covered the tables and the shelves. Perpetual motion machines clicked in rhythm; totally clear clocks showed the movement of every gear as they kept time; and small, motorized replicas of all kinds of planes and space ships covered every surface. They buzzed and whirred softly on his desk. In a glass case above his computer there even was an actual moon rock. A real life artifact from space!

"Wow," I couldn't help but say. "You've got some cool stuff."

Jeronimo nodded his head slightly and scratched his neck. "Thank you, Stephanie." A hive rose under his fingers.

"Serafina," I said.

"What's that?" Jeronimo asked.

"Serafina. That's my name, Serafina. Not Stephanie."

Jeronimo squinted his eyes as if confused and quickly began shuffling paper on his desk. "So it is."

I smiled.

Jeronimo sat back in his chair and tilted his head to the right. "It has come to my attention that I may have been short-sighted in this matter."

I frowned, not knowing what issue he was referring to. "I beg your pardon."

Jeronimo closed his eyes and took a deep breath. "Upon further investigation, we have uncovered a ... a ... a very bad situation." He scratched his neck again with his gloved hands.

I watched him. "Whatever I did, Jeronimo, I can assure you that I am totally sorry and I—"

He held up a gloved finger. "I should be the one

apologizing"—he shuffled his paper once more—"Serafina."

I gasped. What exactly was he apologizing for?

"I understand there was a situation that developed after the original invention presentation where you became the victim of some bullying." He tilted his head again and gave me a sympathetic gaze. "Something like that could make anyone a little queasy."

I pressed my lips together in a tiny, painful line. I felt my chin begin to quiver.

Jeronimo looked at my chin and stood up. "You see this?" he said as he held up both of his gloved hands. "It's 90 degrees outside, and I'm wearing skiing gloves. You know why?"

I shook my head.

"I'm a germaphobe. Do you know what a germaphobe is, Serafina?"

Now it was my turn to tilt my head. "Kind of," I said.

He nodded his head. "You know what one of the least cool things to be in elementary school is?" He didn't even wait for me to answer this time. "A germaphobe. You can't be a normal elementary school kid and be a germaphobe." He scratched his arms. "I hate germs so much that I wouldn't eat at school. I wouldn't share my crayons, and I never, ever went to the bathroom." He turned and looked out the window. "You know what happens when you hold it all day, every day?" He rocked back on his heels. "Eventually you break, like a dam. You pee-pee all over yourself right in front of your class."

I watched Jeronimo as he closed his eyes, obviously thinking about his old memories. It was strange to me to see such an icon, a master of all science, telling me something so personal. Even weirder was the fact that he was telling me about something so embarrassing like peeing in his pants. A few days before, he was piloting a jet-powered table.

"After I peed in front of all my classmates, my mom tried to think of a way for me to be able to do things like use the bathroom without having to actually touch anything. So she bought me a pair of gloves." He looked at the gloves he was wearing. "I've been wearing them ever since."

"But you haven't worn your gloves every day," I said. "I saw you in the cafeteria yesterday without them."

Jeronimo slowly nodded his head. "Yes. Most days I don't need the gloves. I've gotten some help from therapists and some really close friends, and now I can be basically a normal person. But that has only been in the past 10 or so years. I'm 40." He shoved his hands into his pocket. "Until I was 30, I wore gloves everywhere. It didn't matter where I was—school, church, soccer, the mall, the movies, on dates. If I ever got those."

I looked at my hands in my lap. "I'm sorry," I said.

Jeronimo quickly turned around. "No, Serafina. Don't be sorry. You don't have to feel sorry for me. I'm fine. In fact, I'm better than fine. I'm living my dream. I have always wanted to go into space, and here I am." He threw his hands in the air. "I'm going to Mars!" he exclaimed. "My point, in telling you all of this, is that I understand. I understand what it means to be different."

I blinked.

"And to be made fun of for being different." He paused. "Kids used to call me 'the gloved wonder'. They also liked to call me the 'kitten with the mittens'." He took a deep breath. "And 'test tube baby'."

"Test tube baby?" I asked.

Jeronimo shook his head. "Something with germs and test tubes ... I don't know. The point is no one called me by my real name. They teased me all the time about hating germs and peeing in my pants and crying when the older guys dunked my head in the toilet."

"That sounds horrible," I said.

Jeronimo nodded. "It was. What was even worse was this game they used to play called 'hit the mitt'. A group of five or so guys would make it their mission to steal my gloves. It wasn't too hard because, as you can see, I'm not the biggest guy around. I'm no body builder. And to make matters worse, once they got my gloves off, I started getting all crazy with my fear about germs. It would throw me into a tizzy. I would start to panic, which made me cry, and those boys would just laugh and laugh. They loved it. The more I cried, the more they laughed. It was miserable."

I looked down at the floor. "It sounds like it."

"It's why I grew the mohawk. So those bullies would stop focusing on my gloves. It was a lot harder to make fun of a boss-green mohawk." He ran a glove across his hair.

I laughed at that.

Jeronimo came to the chair right next to me and sat down. "The point is that I survived it, and you will, too. In the end, it made me who I am. Sure, I'm a dork, and I love geeky things like rockets and jet engines, but guess what. I'm the best at it! And I love what I'm doing!"

I smiled at Jeronimo. "Thanks," I said.

Jeronimo smiled, too. "I'm sorry we didn't know. I just wish you would have told someone what was happening."

I lowered my eyes.

He was silent for a few beats. "You know, you still broke the rules, but it sounds like it was happening under some pretty serious stress."

I looked at him again.

Jeronimo narrowed his eyes. "But, of course, that doesn't make it right. You know, breaking the rules and all." He leaned forward in his chair. "I may be a lot better with the whole germ thing, but I can't stand vomiting." He shuddered. "I haven't made up my mind on what the consequences should be. I need to think about this."

I nodded my head.

"I just wanted to make sure you're okay," he said and patted my back. "Space is important, but you are more important than any mission."

I looked down at the ground trying to reconcile my feelings with what Jeronimo was saying. Of course, I did feel bad about breaking the contraband food rule, but I felt even worse about Ida.

The week had been rough. I had never been put in a situation quite like the one with Ida. Ida the awful. Ida the cruel. Ida the hammer. She had not only heckled and bullied me in front of the entire space adventure group, but she had gotten her band of lemmings to join in. All week, I had felt like there was hardly anywhere to turn. She had shirts made for goodness sakes!

Of course, I did have my friends, my brand new friends, Taffy and Padma and Emmanuel, who were so different and interesting and loyal. They never turned their backs on me. The entire week, they had been right beside me, helping me though that awful situation with kind words and encouragement and contraband food. One night, when I had been feeling particularly low, they even snuck me outside to watch a meteor shower and eat a box of Twinkies. I love meteor showers! And Twinkies! They did something nice for me, something to make me feel better.

I also had so many people who cared about me at home, like my parents and my friends. Aunt Celeste cared so much she had taken time from discovering the meaning of life just to speak to me.

"Are you okay, Serafina?" Jeronimo asked, snapping me back into reality.

I smiled. "I'm gonna be."

I thought about all the people who did care about me. Maybe I had spent too much time worrying about a person who was most likely never going to like me. For some reason, Ida Hammer hated me and was determined to let me know just how much she despised me. I wasn't sure I could ever change that. I wasn't sure if it even mattered to me. I had never seen Ida be very nice to anyone. I didn't even know if she had friends. I was, however, sure of the fact that there were lots of people like Taffy and Georgia and Aunt Celeste who did care about me. They deserved my time and attention a lot more than Ida Hammer ever would.

He nodded and grinned his horsey, tooth grin. "I know," he said.

CHAPTER TWELVE

I stood outside waiting for my parents to arrive for the awards ceremony. I wore a pea green sundress speckled with dancing pink flamingos that Georgia had lent me.

The dress was hideous, but Georgia thought it was wonderful. In fact, she had insisted that I take it because it was so "amazingly adorable" and was perfect for my "color palette". She must have been insane, either that or she was legally blind. I'm not sure what color palette I had that complemented this shade of green, but it must have been awful. This green was the same shade as the Jello they served in the cafeteria on wilted lettuce leaves.

I stared at one of the flamingos that looked like he was dancing a samba and thought about the ceremony. I knew that I wouldn't win the contest. Ida had made that fact terribly, horribly, painfully, embarrassingly clear. But I still wanted to make it onto the junior astronaut development program, and I felt like I had a good chance.

"My little hyacinth!" I heard a woman's voice yell.

An arm decorated in about a thousand jingly bracelets shot out from the window of a dirty minivan.

"Aunt Celeste!" I yelled as I ran toward Dad's van. "You came!"

As the window rolled down, I heard her favorite song, "People are Strange", playing on the radio.

"Of course I came, my little begonia," she said.

She kissed my cheek as I came to the window.

"Hi, Mom. Hi, Dad," I said. I waved ever so slightly.

"Well, thanks for noticing," Mom said. "I mean, I don't want to steal the spotlight from your favorite person or anything."

Celeste rolled her eyes. "Oh, Charlotte. Your energy is so negative. So passive aggressive."

Mom rolled her eyes.

"I thought you were in Sedona," I said.

Aunt Celeste smoothed her long hair. "Oh I was, my dear periwinkle, but I decided that I should be here tonight. I mean how could I miss out on something as wonderful as robot camp." She adjusted the blue, round sunglasses on her face.

I shook my head.

"Soccer camp?"

I shook it again.

"Kindergarten graduation?" she said, smiling like a cat and peering at me over her shades.

"Aunt Celeste," I wailed. "You know this is Musgrave Space Adventure!"

She nodded dutifully. "Of course I do."

"So. Did you find out the meaning of life?" I asked.

Aunt Celeste nodded. "Of course I did, my sweet

violet."

My parents turned their heads toward her and their eyebrows rose, as if they also were interested.

"The meaning of life?" Mom asked.

Aunt Celeste sat silently, blinking her eyes and fiddling with her bracelets.

"So?" I moaned impatiently.

She looked up with an innocent grin. "Oh! You want the answer?"

"Yes!" we all shouted at once.

Aunt Celeste laughed. "Ah yes, the secret of life."

"Come on, sis. Enough with the theatrics," Mom said.

Aunt Celeste waved her hand like a queen dismissing a servant. "Have patience, Charlotte."

"I can't stand it anymore!" Dad said.

Aunt Celeste smiled once again. "The secret to life, my darling little Serafina is ..."

"Is what?" I asked. My whole body twitched in anticipation.

"—just be yourself, your wonderful, sweet self. Don't let anyone or anything change you. No matter what happens. Always be you."

CHAPTER THIRTEEN

My friends and I sat with the other kids in the front of the auditorium. Everyone was dressed in our best clothes. Boys wore suits and ties. Girls wore fluffy dresses that looked like desserts. Well, all the girls except Ida.

Ida wore a sparkling jumpsuit and tall sparkling boots. She looked beautiful. She looked perfect. Of course, she needed to look perfect for when she accepted her award this evening.

She caught me looking at her, and she narrowed her eyes into little slits.

I looked down at my feet to avoid her gaze, and I sighed. I'd done it again. I was wearing two mismatching shoes: one yellow high top and one soccer cleat.

I don't even remember packing my cleats, I thought. I turned my foot and noticed a label stuck to the side. It read, "Property of Serafina Marina Sterling."

I smiled. "Georgia," I whispered.

"What's that?" Padma asked. "Did you say

something?"

I shook my head.

Ida, who was sitting in the row in front of us, turned around. "Are you talking to yourself now?" she asked. "The stress must be getting to you. You probably aren't cut out for something as competitive as Space Adventure. You probably wouldn't cut it as an astronaut. Maybe you need a hug." She laughed her evil-villain laugh and her lemmings joined in, cackling and snickering at my expense.

"Don't worry about her, Sera," Taffy said.

We all stood and moved away from Ida and her fans.

"If you ignore her, she will eventually leave you alone," Padma said.

Emmanuel nodded in agreement. "That's right. People like her never get too far."

"Are you serious?" I moaned. "Look at her. She's like a rock star. And you know she's going to win tonight. I just don't understand why she can't leave me alone. What did I ever do to her?"

Emmanuel frowned sympathetically. "You don't know who is going to win. For all we know, you could be the winner."

I took a deep breath. "I'm just ready to forget about Ida. I want to have a good time tonight. Besides, we find out who makes the team tonight. How many spots are there?"

"Ten," Taffy said and smiled.

"I bet we all get a spot!" Emmanuel said excitedly.

Padma smiled and giggled. "I hope so!"

Suddenly, we heard a loud tapping on the microphone. It was Jeronimo. He stood on the stage in an ordinary pair of jeans and a t-shirt. No space suit that night, but he was still wearing his ski gloves. I could still see the itchy, red bumps that speckled his arms and neck.

He scratched the side of his face. "Due to the unfortunate events that occurred this morning, I have decided to dispense with the pomp and circumstance for this evening's ceremony."

The microphone squealed as he adjusted the stand.

"I had a speech prepared, but unfortunately it was damaged as I was being hosed down after my ride this morning."

Ida giggled softly.

Taffy looked at me and rolled her eyes.

"So I've decided to speak from the heart this evening."

A slow clap began from a few parents. In a matter of seconds, the entire crowd was loudly applauding.

"Way to go, Jeronimo!" kids and parents shouted.

Jeronimo smiled a weary smile as he touched the side of his mohawk with his glove.

He continued. "I came here this week with the intention of teaching these young astronauts about science. I also wanted to teach them about leadership, about how to make things happen. I wanted to show them how I have grown my own dream, a dream about reaching the stars, into a reality. Instead, I got barfed on and then had a panic attack."

A few nervous parents laughed. They probably

had no idea that Jeronimo had actually had a panic attack.

"Anyway," he said clearing his throat. "What I found out is that I learned something from these kids. I was forced to reflect upon my own path and what factors led me to the place that I am today. When I thought about it, I realized it was never the science or the stock price or the awards that made me successful. I was reminded about the simple formula to success. A formula that is very easy to forget once you have already made it."

Ida shifted in her seat, reflecting light from her sparkling outfit. "Let's do this," she said impatiently. "I'm ready to get my award."

"The formula I am talking about comes from here." He touched his heart with a gloved hand. "To be successful, you must first never give up. It's called persistence. Don't ever lose sight of your dreams and don't stop until you get there. It's that simple, but here's the catch. There are lots of ways of getting there and a lot of them involve people because we live in a world with lots of other people. We are part of a community, a scientific discipline, a world. You either can work with people and add to their lives or you can simply run over them. Disregard their feelings. Treat them like they are collateral damage. It's important that what we do in our lives adds to those around us. Because, in the end, all we have is each other. The idea leads me to the second and most important part of my formula, which is—"

Ida sighed. "Boring!"

"—compassion," he said. "You have to care about others." He scratched the side of his face. "Without compassion you will be a lonely person. You can, and probably will, win awards and achieve big things if you're smart and determined. But how much are those things going to mean when you have no one to share them with? Eventually, all of those people who have helped you achieve by doing things like serving you breakfast or being a structural engineering expert won't be there."

My friends and I looked at each other. Everyone smiled.

"And that's it. To be a successful scientist, you must be persistent and compassionate. It's that simple. Those are the kind of astronauts I'm looking for."

Applause slowly grew among the crowd.

Jeronimo pulled a sheet of paper from his pocket. "With that being said, I want to move onto one of the most important parts of the evening: the awards."

"Finally!" Ida groaned.

"She's just miserable," Taffy whispered.

"First, I would like to present the award for best original invention."

I sunk in my chair. "Well, I guess it's time for Ida to be happy again. I mean, after she accepts her award and everything."

"Space travel is not just about getting there and back. Of course, we can't really go anywhere without a solid ship, but there are lots of other considerations that happen to people when they spend months in space."

Taffy furrowed her brows. "Didn't you say that her fidget spinner wasn't actually meant for zero gravity? On the vomit comet, didn't you say that it spun out of control once you guys hit zero g?"

I tilted my head to the side, recalling the unfortunate ride that morning. "That's right," I said. "It didn't actually stay put once all our gravity went away. It went spinning like a top through the air."

"One of the most important factors is the mental health of astronauts, but that also is one of the most overlooked aspects of space travel. We get so caught up in thrust and load that we forget about the astronauts themselves," Jeronimo said.

Taffy squinted. "Then why would she win the award if her invention didn't even work?"

"We had only one junior astronaut who considered and created a device that took into account the psychology of space travelers. That junior astronaut is Serafina Sterling, with her hugging machine."

Taffy covered her mouth. "It's you, Serafina! You won!"

Just like on the vomit comet, the gravity seemed to disappear. I felt like I was floating. I felt Taffy and Emmanuel and Padma pushing me toward the stage but it was all in slow motion. It was like I was in zero g. Only this time I wasn't.

This time I was in regular Earth gravity, in the auditorium of the Musgrave Space Institute. I had just won an award for my hugging machine. The same hugging machine that Ida had ridiculed. The same hugging machine that I felt ashamed of even though

I had once thought it was a wicked cool invention.

A woman's voice shouted from the back, "Boooooooom!" Her voice, much like my motion, was being distorted by the surreal zero-gravity feeling. "What do you think about her now?" The sound came in slow waves. "Boooooom! In your face!"

It was Aunt Celeste. She was doing an obnoxious dance in front of all the space adventurers with her hands behind her head and her hips swinging wildly. "That's my niece, people, and don't you forget iiiiiiiiiiiiit!"

I winced as I watched her do the funky beaver dance.

I saw Mom run in half speed, also being affected by the strange local gravity, toward her sister. It was like those movies where they slow everything down for dramatic effect. She jumped on Aunt Celeste's back as she yelled, "Celeste, these are childreeeeennnnn! Quit making a fool of yourseeeeeeelf!"

I passed Mom and Aunt Celeste as they wrestled, but slowly, in that dreamy kind of way.

Jeronimo was on the stage, smiling and holding something. It looked like a trophy. It was shaped like a moon rock, all dimpled and lumpy, just like the actual moon rock I had seen in his office.

"Congratulations, Serafinaaaaaa." His voice was slow and deep. The gravity had been magically sucked away from him as well. A slow, lazy curl formed on his lips. He was smiling his giant horsey tooth grin at me.

I smiled and walked slowly onto the stage.

I heard a commotion from behind. I thought it would be Aunt Celeste still taunting the other space adventurers but what I saw was Ida, all seven feet of her, raising slowly and running toward the back doors. "Not faaaaaaaaair!" she shouted.

I looked back toward Jeronimo. He didn't seem to notice. He placed the moon rock into my hands. "Do you want to make a speeeeeeeech?" he asked.

I blinked slowly, still caught in this slow-motion reality. It was my dream coming true. Then all at once I snapped back. Gravity returned and the speed of life became normal once again. "No," I said. "I need to find Ida." I ran out the back doors after her.

It didn't take me long to find her. She sat in the dorm wing against a wall. She was crunched into a ball and crying. Black streaks of makeup flowed down her face.

She must not have known I was there because as soon as I got near her, she jerked like she was startled.

"What do you want, you freak?" she asked as she wiped her eyes.

I slid down the wall and sat beside her. "Are you okay?" I asked.

"Of course I'm not okay, you freak! I lost the most important contest of my life to a basic girl and her basic hugging machine." Snot ran out of her nose as she continued to sob.

"Look," I said. "I didn't come here to listen to this. I just wanted to make sure you were alright." I stood up and began to walk away.

"Wait!" Ida shouted as she rose to her feet. "Don't

go."

I turned around and studied her face.

"I'm sorry," she said in a tiny voice, a voice that didn't even sound like her own.

The look on my face must have betrayed how surprised I was because she said, "I know you're shocked. I am, too. I never apologize, not to anyone or anything. It's just"—she paused and wiped her eyes—"it's just that I didn't mean to hurt you. I took things too far."

I took a few steps toward her and looked up at her red, slimy face. She really needed a tissue. "Why? Why did you do that to me? What did I ever do to you? Was it because I accidentally bumped into you on the first day?"

Ida rubbed her snotty nose and shook her head. "No."

"Then why?" I pleaded. "Why do you hate me?"

Ida gasped. "I don't hate you, Serafina. Of course, I can see why you would think that. But no, I don't hate you. It's just that I don't like you."

I threw my arms in the air. "But why?"

Ida sighed. "It was the hugging machine."

"But I won! It wasn't basic. Jeronimo loved it," I said.

"I know!" Ida yelled. "That's the point! I heard Jeronimo gushing about your invention as I was setting up my pyrotechnics before the show. He was saying how original and unconventional your device was. He said that he was impressed that someone as young as you was able to comprehend something as complex as human emotional needs."

"What?" I was in total shock at her confession.

"It's true," she said. "And I was so bummed. I needed to—no, I *had* to—win this contest, and I just couldn't let you win. I had to neutralize you. I had to figure out a way to break you down. So, you know. The rest is history."

I put my hands on the side of my face. "But you made me miserable, Ida. I wanted to quit. I felt terrible about myself. I was this close"— I put my thumb and forefinger about a millimeter apart to show Ida just how close I was—"to calling my parents and begging them to take me home."

She began to cry. "I'm sorry, Serafina," she moaned. "I just have all this pressure. I mean I have tutors, and coaches, and a social media manager, and scientific advisors, and my parents. My parents are just so ... just so ... demanding! It's like I can't make them happy. Ever." Her small cries turned into shoulder-shaking sobs.

I walked over to Ida and stood on my tippy toes. I opened my arms and squeezed her in a really tight, really big bear hug. "I'm sorry, Ida. I'm sorry you have all that pressure."

She laid her head on my shoulder and continued to cry.

"Come on," I said. "Let's go see if we're gonna be astronauts."

EPILOGUE

In the end, all of my friends made Jeronimo's junior astronaut development program—even Ida. That meant that one day we would all be on a rocket ship, hurdling toward Mars.

I hadn't thought I was going to make it, not just in the space adventure but also through that week. It was one of the most difficult experiences I had ever been through, what with the bullying and the t-shirts and the awful things that Ida said about me. While the shirts and all that hash tagging were super harsh, the worst part of the whole week was that I had believed the things that Ida said.

I had believed that my invention was terrible and that I was a totally unworthy scientist. But that wasn't true. Not at all.

Ida had done all of those things because of her own insecurities. In secret, Ida had thought I was awesome. She thought I was a good scientist. She thought that I could make it as an astronaut. She thought that I was so good that she'd had to destroy me.

The truth was that I *was* good enough. And I realized that day—the day I became a junior astronaut at the Musgrave Space Institute—that just being me, Serafina Marina Sterling, was the secret to life.

All the way home, I sat in the back of the van clutching my moon rock and hearing that weird, hippie song of Aunt Celeste's playing in my head. People *are* strange. They're kind of like a Rubik's cube that's made out of Jello. And once you finally think you have all the colors lined up and you're about to slide the final block into place, the whole stinking thing melts in your hand.

But there is something else that's true about people, too. While people are strange, we're also the same in a lot of ways. We all have fears and insecurities and anxieties and hopes and dreams and plans for our future. And because of that, it's a little easier to figure each other out.

FROM THE WEBLOG OF
SERAFINA STERLING

www.SerafinaLovesScience.com

Serafina's Scientific Stylings

Entry #1—Newton: The Man, The Beehive, The Laws

I'm trying this whole blogging thing because it seems like to be relevant you need a web presence. You need to hashtag and get that app that puts dog-ears on your head. I firmly believe that any serious scientist doesn't need to have animated dog-ears to reach the public, but I do concede that I must keep up with the times. Therefore, I'll be using my dad's credit card to register my URL and my Wednesday afternoons to muse about various scientific concepts.

During a recent trip to Musgrave Space Institute, I was re-introduced to some basic physical laws that seem to have more application than just describing the principles of motion. These laws were described by none other than Sir Isaac Newton. (My fifth grade science teacher, Mr. Gobbler, who interestingly had a small side business of buying and selling Thanksgiving memorabilia, first showed me the world of Newton during our space unit.) Newton can totally wear the crown of scientific royalty, not just because of his super voluminous hair, but because he stands tall among the historical pack of mathematicians, physicists, astronomers, and theorists like Einstein, Galileo, and Copernicus. Newton's work laid the foundation for modern scientific understanding.

Sir Isaac was born sometime between Christmas Day in 1641 and January 4 in 1642. And even though his hair was glorious, Newton wasn't all about the glory. He cared about knowing how the world worked.

Before the famous apple-smacking incident, Newton was getting down with math and science by inventing calculus, dabbling in advanced geometry, developing theories of light and how it creates color, building advanced telescopes to observe the planets and their movements, and basically striving to understand how the most basic components of our universe operate.

Only later, as legend has it, was Newton out in an apple orchard and clobbered by some falling fruit. The fruit prompted the following thoughts: "Why me? Why my hair? Especially after I just got this perm!" Well, I may have embellished those thoughts, but the way the apple fell did leave him questioning. Newton wondered, "Why did the apple fall in this particular way?" This pondering led him to identify a universal force, a force we know today as gravity.

Newton saw that gravity was an invisible attraction that the Earth held over objects. He saw that anything that had mass was inevitably attracted toward the center of the Earth. Newton also saw that gravity was consistent, predictable, and measurable. Mass was attracted to mass. Based upon these observations, three universal laws were developed that forever changed the way we see the world:

Law #1—This law states that an object at rest tends to stay at rest while an object in motion tends to stay in motion. This means that if there is no outside force acting upon object A, then the motion of object A will remain constant. Same goes for an object that is at rest.

This is how those perpetual motion machines work. I'm sure you all have that one crazy uncle or weird neighbor who has those things clicking all day and all night. The balls move back and forth, slamming into one another, and it seems like it will never end—because it won't. Once the net motion has been established for an object, it will remain constant. We call this inertia.

Before Newton, people didn't know how or why objects moved the way they did. They simply assumed that it was a natural part of the object, something that was built in. Now, not only do we know that there is a universal law governing how objects move based upon their inertia, but we also can predict that movement. This is important when building things like spaceships, satellites, and even minivans.

Law #2—Newton's second law states that the change in the motion of an object is directly proportion to the external force applied to the object. Mathematically speaking, we represent this law using the following equation:

Force = Mass (how much does it weigh?) * Acceleration (how fast is it going?)

The change or momentum of the object can be determined using this equation. We have to understand this change when making things (like spaceships and rockets) fly.

Law #3—The third and final law is probably the most famous and the most quotable. Newton stated that for every action there is an equal and opposite reaction. This means that if object A exerts a force on object B, that force will be applied equally back at object A. I like to call that the tit for tat, quid pro quo, you-get-what-you-give law.

This principle describes the phenomenon that allows us to lift giant heaps of metal off the ground and into space. Have you ever seen a space shuttle launch? Did you notice all that gnarly fire and exhaust that comes out of the end of that thruster? This isn't just for show.

All of that energy is being directed at the launch pad. The launch pad is in turn applying an equal force back at the rocket, creating lift for the ship. Pretty amazing stuff!

Newton and his manly beehive still reveal basic

truths about the universe nearly 300 years later. His scientific stylings showed us how to understand and predict the way objects move on Earth as governed by gravity. This has allowed us to create mass transportation, build airplanes, and even land a man on the moon. All because of one falling apple and one manly beehive.

It's amazing how one person so long ago can create an impact so far reaching. I think about Newton and his impact and wonder if I will ever be able to do the same. Who knows? I might be one fruit tree away from discovering the truth about dark matter or cataloguing the DNA of Bigfoot. In the meantime, I am grateful for scientific pioneers and the path they have forged in understanding the world. I am also grateful for the ability to continue to learn about the world every day.

Stay curious, kids. Maybe next time, I'll be blogging about you.

Serafina Marina Sterling, future Ph.D.

Weblog Sources:

https://www.grc.nasa.gov/www/k-12/airplane/newton.html

https://www.khanacademy.org/science/physics/forces-newtons-laws/newtons-laws-of-motion/a/what-is-newtons-first-law

IDA HAMMER'S ZERO-GRAVITY FIDGET SPINNER!

What you will need:

- One fidget spinner
- An enclosed fan with a flat surface
- Paper
- Duct tape
- Scissors

Step One:

Find your most trusty, dusty fidget spinner. Make sure all the bearings are spinning properly by giving it a whirl or two.

Step Two:

Use your aeronautical knowledge to fashion some basic propellers for your fidget spinner. You will use construction paper, tape, and lots of trial and error to create and tape a propeller to each of the three fidget arms. You will want to make your propellers each about 0.5-1 inch in length. (This is where the trial and error comes into action. You'll find one length might work better than another.)

Step Three:

Lift off! Get your enclosed fan laying flat on the floor or table with the air discharge pointed toward the ceiling. Set the fan on its highest possible setting. Begin to spin your modified fidget spinner over the shaft of air. If you have adequately engineered a righteous set of propellers, you should be witnessing your fidget spinner defy gravity! Well, it's really just getting lots of upward thrust, but it totally looks like it's floating!

Step Four:

If at first you don't succeed, try, try again. Experiment with the lengths of the propellers to achieve maximum lift. See if you and your friends can float the highest or the longest.

About Cara Bartek, Ph.D.

I love science! More importantly, I love helping kids develop a passion for science. This world is a big, scary, and confusing place sometimes, but the good news is we can rely on some seriously important things to help us through, like faith and family and friends and education! Education helps open the door to opportunities and worlds we may not otherwise experience. It actually makes the world a bigger place! But we have to feed our education, and we do that by scratching our curiosity. Curiosity is the key that helps our brains and our hearts grow. I created the Serafina Loves Science! series to show that science is not only interesting but also relatable. I hope to make the world bigger and brighter and way more interesting through science!

I live in Texas with my husband, Matt, and my two little girls, Caroline and Penelope. I also am compelled to mention my two furry children, Beetle and Bob. Bob is a weiner-beagle (think overstuffed sausage with long legs,) and Beetle is a possible pit/raccoon mix; genetic tests are still pending. We also have a couple of hissing cockroaches named Shimmer and Shine that live in a pink terrarium on our kitchen island. Matt and I own an agricultural business that keeps us busy and sunburnt! Some of my favorite things to do are charting stars with my kids, spending time on the beach checking out the sea turtles and pelicans, reading (my favorite book is *A Wrinkle in Time*), and writing. The rest is history! Visit me at www.carabartek.com.

Did you enjoy this book?

Check out all the books in the Serafina Loves Science! series, including the second book, *Quantum Quagmire*!

Visit www.absolutelovepublishing.com for the latest releases. And be sure to leave your review on any online platform!

About Absolute Love Publishing

Absolute Love Publishing is an independent book publisher devoted to creating and publishing books that promote goodness in the world.

www.AbsoluteLovePublishing.com

Young Adult & Children's Books by Absolute Love Publishing

Dear One, Be Kind by Jennifer Farnham
This beautiful children's book takes young children on a journey of harmony and empathy. Using rhyme and age-appropriate language and imagery, *Dear One, Be Kind* illustrates how children can embrace feelings of kindness and love for everyone they meet, even when others are seemingly hurtful. By revealing the unseen message behind common childhood experiences, the concept of empathy is introduced, along with a gentle knowledge of our interconnectedness and the belief that, through kindness, children have the power to change their world. Magically illustrated with a soothing and positive message, this book is a joy for children and parents alike!

Different
Twelve-year-old Izzy wants to be like everyone else, but she has a secret. She isn't weird or angry, like some of the kids at school think. Izzy has Tourette syndrome. Hiding outbursts and tics from her classmates is hard enough, but when a new girl arrives, Izzy's fear of losing her best friend makes Izzy's symptoms worse. And when she sees her crush act suspiciously, runaway thoughts take root inside of her. As the pressure builds and her world threatens to spin out of control, Izzy must face her fear and reveal her secret, whatever the costs.

Authentic and perceptive, *Different* shines a light on the delicate line of a child's hopes and fears and inspires us all to believe that perhaps we are not so different after all.

The Adima Chronicles by Steve Schatz

Adima Rising
For millennia, the evil Kroledutz have fed on the essence of humans and clashed in secret with the Adima, the light weavers of the universe. Now, with the balance of power shifting toward darkness, time is running out. Guided by a timeless Native American spirit, four teenagers from a small New Mexico town discover they have one month to awaken their inner power and save the world.

Rory, Tima, Billy, and James must solve four ancient challenges by the next full moon to awaken a mystical portal and become Adima. If they fail, the last threads of light will dissolve, and the universe will be lost forever. Can they put aside their fears and discover their true natures before it's too late?

Adima Returning
The Sacred Cliff is crumbling and with it the Adima way of life! Weakened by the absence of their beloved friend James, Rory, Tima, and Billy must battle time and unseen forces to unite the greatest powers of all dimensions in one goal. They must move the Sacred Cliff before it traps all Adima on Earth—and apart from the primal energy of the Spheres—forever!

Aided by a surprising and timeless maiden, the three light-weaving teens travel across the planes of existence to gain help from the magical creatures who guard the Adima's most powerful objects, the Olohos. There is only one path to success: convince the guardians to help. Fail and the Cliff dissolves, destroying the once-eternal Spheres and the interdimensional light weavers known as Adima.

Like the exciting adventures of *Adima Rising*, the second spellbinding book of The Adima Chronicles, *Adima Returning*, will have your senses reeling right up until its across-worlds climax. Will conscious creation and the bonds of friendship be enough to fight off destructive forces and save the world once again?

The Soul Sight Mysteries by Janet McLaughlin

Haunted Echo
Sun, fun, toes in the sand, and daydreams about her boyfriend back home. That's what teen psychic Zoey Christopher expects for her spring break on an exotic island. But from the moment she steps foot onto her best friend Becca's property, Zoey realizes the island has other plans: chilling drum beats, a shadowy ghost, and a mysterious voodoo doll.

Zoey has always seen visions of the future, but when she arrives at St. Anthony's Island to vacation among the jet set, she has her first encounter with a bona fide ghost. Forced to uncover the secret behind the girl's untimely death, Zoey quickly realizes that trying to solve the case will thrust her into mortal danger—and into the arms of a budding crush. Can Zoey put the tormented spirit's soul to rest without her own wild emotions haunting her?

Fireworks
Dreams aren't real. Psychic teen Zoey Christopher knows

the difference between dreams and visions better than anyone, but ever since she and her best friend returned from spring vacation, Zoey's dreams have been warning her that Becca is in danger. But a dream isn't a vision—right?

Besides, Zoey has other things to worry about, like the new, cute boy in school. Dan obviously has something to hide, and he won't leave Zoey alone—even when it causes major problems with Josh, Zoey's boyfriend. Is it possible he knows her secret?

Then, one night, Becca doesn't answer any of Zoey's texts or calls. She doesn't answer the next morning either. When Zoey's worst fears come true, her only choice is to turn to Dan, whom she discovers has a gift different from her own but just as powerful. Is it fate? Will using their gifts together help them save Becca, or will the darkness win?

Discover what's real and what's just a dream in *Fireworks*, book two of the Soul Sight Mysteries!

Serafina Loves Science! by Cara Bartek, Ph.D.

Cosmic Conundrum
In *Cosmic Conundrum*, sixth grader Serafina Sterling finds herself accepted into the Ivy League of space adventures for commercial astronauts, where she'll study with Jeronimo Musgrave, a famous and flamboyant scientist who brought jet-engine minivans to the suburbs. Unfortunately, Serafina also meets Ida Hammer, a 12-year-old superstar of science who has her own theorem, a Nobel-Prize-winning mother, impeccable

fashion sense—*and* a million social media followers. Basically, she's everything Serafina's not. Or so Serafina thinks.

Even in an anti-gravity chamber, Serafina realizes surviving junior astronaut training will take more than just a thorough understanding of Newton's Laws. She'll have to conquer her fear of public speaking, stick to the rules, and overcome the antics of Ida. How will Serafina survive this cosmic conundrum?

Quantum Quagmire
Serafina suspects something is wrong when her best friend, Tori Copper, loses interest in their most cherished hobbies: bug hunting and pizza nights. When she learns Tori's parents are getting a divorce and that Tori's mom is moving away, Serafina vows to discover a scientific solution to a very personal problem so that Tori can be happy again. But will the scientific method, a clever plan, and a small army of arachnids be enough to reunite Tori's parents? When the situation goes haywire, Serafina realizes she has overlooked the smallest, most quantum of details. Will love be the one challenge science can't solve?

Join Serafina in another endearing adventure in book two of the Serafina Loves Science! series.

97104904R00069

Made in the USA
San Bernardino, CA
21 November 2018